LOST BOY

by

Edward Love Johnson

DEDICATION

It gives me great pleasure to dedicate this book to the memory of MACIE WILSON FRYE, a dear friend whose great faith in God and Prayer has been an inspiration to me in my writing.

PART I

CHAPTER 1

Far up in the wilds of the Monongahela, somewhere beyond the swirling waters of the Song Bird River, and farther still, to the towering peaks of the fabled Allegheny Highlands, which formed the core of the mythical Monongahela National Forest, a startling series of events was soon to unfold.

Forty feet up, on the face of a steep boulder strewn peak, a she-panther came out of a deep cavity that knifed sharply into the face of a gray lichen covered sandstone cliff. The tip of her long tail twitched as her amber eyes surveyed the valley floor.

A fox squirrel came out of the wooded hill on the far side of the valley, found something in the scrubby growth to nibble on, then meandered across to the edge of the slope below the panther's lair. She lost interest in the squirrel when he climbed up a towering chestnut oak and began searching for nuts to open for breakfast.

Farther down the valley, a woodchuck poked his head out of his den beneath a huge boulder. He stood erect, surveying the area. Apparently, he decided that all was clear, for he began to feed on the weeds along the side of the hard packed game trail. Everything seemed normal.

1

A soft breeze, filled with the freshness of early autumn, and tinted with the faint odor of a fading fall aster, filtered up through the trees. It brought nothing to fear, but it's slight smell of freshly dropped leaves served as a warning to the hibernators to put on a good layer of fat to nourish them during their long winter's nap.

It was all part of life in the deep wilds of the Monongahela. Another day when the lesser animals fought over food and the greater animals fought over turf.

The creatures of the dark were slipping away to their dens, and those whose eyes required the light of day were taking over.-- Always on the search for food--Always with a watchful eye for predators.

The she-panther gave a soft purr, and a four-month-old kitten came out of the crevice behind her. For a moment he swatted at the black tip of her long tail with a forepaw, then he stood beside her, mimicking her intensity.

The mother caressed the kitten's head with her soft tongue, then swiped down his back where the black kitten spots were fading from his fur, to leave a tawny gray-brown coat that would blend with the forest.

Twice the female panther glanced up at the ledge some four feet above where she stood, and the kitten followed her eyes. The kitten knew that this was where food came from, frequently in the early morning hours. But today, there was no food. Nor had there been any dropped from the ledge the previous two days. So it fell to the mother panther to roust up some meat for the kitten to munch on.

Any growing baby has a stomach that cries out for food on a regular basis.

And members of the cat families were no exception. If anything, they were more demanding.

Unlike most males of his kind, the ancient old panther who had fathered this kitten had no desire to kill his own offspring. Rather, he had chosen to nourish his mate and her young. He had done this faithfully for the past four months. Yet, like all hunters, human and otherwise, there had occasionally been dry spells. And for the last three days the old panther had experienced one.

To the kitten, the old panther had no identity beyond the meat he brought. The kitten had no way of knowing that the great head he frequently saw protruding over the ledge above him belonged to his father. Nor could he know that, to all of the animals of the forest, this supplier of meat was still the King of the Monongahela. This fact remained, even though the old panther had lost some of his agility to age. And, to the residents of Cave Creek Valley, some fifty miles distant, he was still known as the legendary panther, Old Crooked Toe.

None of this mattered to the kitten. He was well fed, his lithe little body had grown strong and supple. Life seemed so perfect for the little panther as he and his mother set off on their daily hunt, walking side by side, the mother drilling her offspring in hunting skills. From his daily hunts with his mother, he was learning the art of survival in a harsh and unforgiving world.

The sun had already found its way down the side of the peak. Bright red and gold leaves filtered down through the crisp autumn air, adding a touch of color to the forest floor about them.

The panthers had travelled only a short distance when the kitten pounced on a katydid that had fallen from a tree limb. He promptly ate it and looked around for more.

Soon they came to a little brook flowing swiftly between two ridges. The kitten saw a frog dive into the water and hide beneath a large brown leaf. His mother had taught the kitten how to flip a leaf and catch the frog before it could hop away. Remembering the lesson, the kitten procured his first serious bite of breakfast.

A red tailed hawk screamed loudly and long as it circled above the forest roof.

The she-panther paused, her eyes flashing about the forest floor. She was not looking for the hawk. She knew where it was. She was looking for any movement, some creature that might be frightened into action, such as a fawn that a mother deer had hidden away while she browsed. But all that the mother panther saw was a pair of fox squirrels give up their hunt for nuts and race to safety. They scurried to a giant black oak tree that towered above the forest, spreading out over the smaller trees. Twenty feet up, they scrambled into a hole. One poked his head out and barked loudly, then withdrew back into the safety of his den.

The panthers followed the brook a short distance. A second frog found it's way into the kitten's hungry little stomach. The hunt was going well.

Or was it?

Soon,they came around to a bold hump on the next ridge. The mother panther paused. From the hump, she could survey the entire ridge and the slopes on either side of the valley. It was a place she came to frequently, for it provided the perfect vantage point to search for the movement of game.

Farther down the valley, she saw a doe break cover and come shyly into the trail. It paused for a moment, then started up the trail toward her. It wasn't running from danger, but grazing. It was finding sufficient feed to keep it moving toward her, toward the waiting she-panther.

Her interest was stirred further when she saw a pair of half-grown fawns break cover, feeding as they followed along behind their mother The she-panther was surveying the bottom of the slopes on both sides of the trail to determine where she could either stalk the deer, or set up an ambush. She realized that it might be easier to ambush the fawns as they tagged along behind their mother, secure in the doe's presence.

The female panther was so intent on what she was planning, that she failed to see two hunters who had come out into the open on the steep slope off to her left. Like her, they too were looking for a kill.

The kitten had wandered away in search of other game, when he heard the loud crack of a rifle. This was a new sound to him, yet he knew at once that it was something to be feared. He heard the dull thud of lead hitting flesh, but had no idea what he was hearing. He turned in time to see his mother rear up and fall over backwards.

For a moment, the kitten froze. He saw his mother's legs flail and then grow still. He watched her blood seep out of her body, and spread across the rock ledge where she lay. The smell of death was in his nostrils, and it engendered a sudden great fear which raced through his little body.

Somehow the kitten knew that the she-panther, the one he had looked to for security and food, was no longer alive. It was his first experience with loss, yet Mother Nature was guiding him.

His mother was gone. Of that he was fully aware. Now he was alone. -- Alone in a harsh world. A land where might was right, and he was the weaker.

CHAPTER 2

A second time the rifle sounded. Dust and little bits of rock flew up from the ledge, stinging the kitten's throat and breast. He leaped back, hesitated a moment, then whirled and ran. It was the only thing he knew to do.

He had no thought of where he was going. He just wanted to get away from the horror, and the strange and frightening sounds that had dealt death to his mother -- get away fast. His little legs pumped, vainly trying to increase his speed.

The kitten had just dived into heavy cover when the third crash of the rifle split the morning air. He continued his flight around the ridge, still running hard, still terribly frightened.

In a split second his entire world had been torn apart. The mother who should be running beside him was not there, nor would she ever be again. Somehow, he knew that. The den on the cliff that had been his security for all of his life, was somewhere behind him. He wasn't sure where. Yet he had no desire to return. He just wanted to get away. Away from these strange new happenings that had shattered his world so suddenly and so completely.

He crossed the next ravine, with another swiftly flowing branch. But he didn't look for frogs. Rather, he attempted to leap the branch and keep running, but his leap fell short. He landed in the middle of the stream and scrambled onto the far bank. He paused long enough to shake the water from his fur, then he looked back to see if anything was following him. He saw nothing, yet the absence of a chaser did nothing to allay the fear that had taken hold of his entire being.

He dashed around to the crest of the adjoining ridge, then turned down the back of the ridge. Before long he found himself just under the crest of the high irregular mountain that formed the eastern wall of the valley his mother had been watching only moments before.

He paused, just long enough to check the forest about him, then continued to run. Only when he was close to a mile from the scene of carnage, did he slow to a walk, because his legs were growing so weary.

A great mountain ash had fallen here, leaving a hole in the forest roof that encouraged a rash of new growth. The kitten dashed into a dense thicket. He wanted only to hide; he was trembling with fear, and he tried to flatten himself down so he could not be seen. His little legs, unused to such long running, trembled violently. He nestled down in the leaves, so that those frightening things that had killed his mother could not get to him.

The sun had already crossed the meridian and was falling away to the west when the kitten stirred. He had not slept, but he had rested. He had never felt so alone; he was still frightened. He had no idea where he was. He only knew he was far from his den, but he was not looking for a way to return there. Yet, right now, how he would have welcomed that big head that had dropped so many large chunks of sweet red meat onto the ledge before his den.

That big head belonged to the only friendly creature left in his limited world. Bereft and friendless, he crept to the edge of the thicket and prepared to face whatever was out there in the world. His world, that world which had been so friendly and fascinating up until the past few frightful hours.

When the kitten came out into the open, he did not run. Instead, he moved cautiously. He had paid close attention to his mother stalking game. He was attempting to mimic her stance, her actions. That was how his mother had put food into his hungry stomach on those days when the big head had failed to appear. And now he was hungry, very hungry, and still very frightened.

He had gone only a short distance from the thicket when he heard a loud shuffling of leaves. He paused, listening, then reared up so he could see what was making so much stir there on the hillside. Then, he saw the two hunters.

He had no way of knowing if these were the ones who had made the great bang that killed his mother. He only knew they looked very big. And they were coming toward him.

He saw one of the hunters point his rifle up toward the top of a tree, and he heard another loud bang like the one that had ended the life of his mother. He slunk down, but continued to watch the two creatures coming toward him.

Something fell out of the tree. When one of the creatures picked it up, the kitten could see that it was one of the squirrels. He realized the squirrel was dead, just like his mother. That loud bang had killed it.

Fear overtook the kitten as the the creatures approached him. They looked bigger as they came nearer. That loud boom was still ringing in his ears. He flattened himself down as low as he could, and crept back into the thicket he had just left. He continued back until he felt he was well concealed.

The two hunters continued on up the mountain past the thicket where the panther kitten lay concealed. They made a lot of noise in the leaves and made noises that sounded strange to him as they talked to each other.

The two paused when they were very close to the thicket and the kitten heard the crash of the rifle again. He stopped breathing. Something fell out of the tree. He saw one of the men pick it up. It was another squirrel, and he knew it was dead.

As the hunters moved away, he could hear their shuffling in the leaves as they continued up to the mountain top. The sound faded away as they went down the other side. But he didn't hear any more blasts from their guns.

It was more than an hour before the panther kitten ventured out of his hiding place. Then he came out with much caution. Once again, he was trying to mimic his mother in her caution.

He began cruising down the back of the long mountain, keeping just under it's irregular, tree studded crest. His eyes and ears were alert to every movement, every sound.

He continued to look toward the top of the mountain where he had last heard the hunters. He didn't want any further association with those creatures and he didn't want to be surprised by them.

A squirrel saw him and raced away to the nearest tree. He did not give chase. But the next one the kitten surprised, he did try to catch. It easily outran him and scooted up the side of a tree, running as fast up the tree as it had run on the ground.

The squirrels were working the leaves everywhere, looking for nuts to bury for winter. So the kitten tried to stalk the squirrel, but he made too much noise in the leaves. That did not work any better than the chase.

A hundred feet farther down, he heard another sound in the dry leaves. He spied a chipmunk searching for fallen nuts. He waited patiently, flattening down in the carpet of leaves like a part of the forest floor. When the little animal was within striking distance, the kitten leaped.

The chipmunk attempted to flee, but the kitten struck it down with a flailing forepaw. He grasped it by the back and held fast. The chipmunk turned it's head and bit him on the lip, but he did not let it go. He held on until the chipmunk's little body grew limp.

The kitten had made his first kill. He wasn't particularly proud of himself, but success did bolster some feeling of accomplishment. He dropped the chipmunk on the ground and stared down at it.

The meat that had routinely been dropped on the lip of the den had always been free of skin, or had the hide pulled back. Likewise, when his mother made a kill, she had always opened it up in some manner. This kill was covered with skin and hair. Where did he start?

Hunger pangs solved the problem for him. He picked up the little creature and started chewing. He ground it up, hide, bones, and meat. He swallowed it all and licked the few drops of blood from the leaves. His stomach was far from full. It was still crying for food, but he had made a start. It gave him a feeling of security in his ability to support himself.

He continued the hunt, moving now with even more caution. He was learning how to set his feet down more gently in the leaves. He didn't have it right just yet, but he was trying.

Twice, he came up to the crest of the mountain and looked down on the other side. That was where the hunters had gone, but he saw none. That side of the mountain was much steeper than the slope he had been following, so he dropped back.

He began a wide swing down the mountain that would point him back to the thicket where he had found shelter. He hoped to find a spring and possibly a frog or two. When he finally did come upon a spring, there was no frog in it, only a lizard. It wasn't his favorite dish but it was food, and that was what he was looking for. He ate it.

From his vantage point on the side of the mountain he was able to see movement on the game trail below him. Twice he saw deer, one running as though it was being chased, but he saw no pursuer. Then he saw a bear. It looked very big. In fact, just the sight of it frightened him. He tried to crouch down among the leaves so he could not be seen.

The bear came up the trail, crossed the little brook that flowed swiftly down the valley and vanished up a draw on the opposite mountain. The ripples of fear running through his little body were now quieted.

Twice he attempted to stalk squirrels hunting nuts on the ground, but failed. He still had not mastered the ability to pick his way quietly through the leaves, but he was trying. He happened on a pair of wood rats scratching for food, making a considerable fuss as they dug into the leaf carpet. But they were alert, frequently rearing up to check for any approaching predator.

The kitten was learning. Experience was proving to be a great teacher. He could now see that directly stalking a quarry was not possible in the heavy carpet of leaves, and the leaves were everywhere.

The rats were scrounging near a great fallen spruce. Possibly their den was under the tree trunk. The kitten dropped back, making a wide half circle. He came in on the opposite side of the log. Caution and stealth were the important elements of stalking and the little panther was a fast learner.

When the kitten peeped over the log, he saw the two rats coming toward him. Apparently they had heard him and were racing to their shelter under the fallen tree. He had to act quickly. The kitten leaped onto the log, then leaped again to meet the rats. As he came down he caught one of the animals with his paw.

Again he was learning. His lip was still smarting from the chipmunk bite. So he bit into the rat just back of the head, where it had no chance of biting him. He bore down, not releasing his hold until the rat was dead.

Again, he looked at all of the fur and skin. But he did not hesitate this time. He promptly attacked the carcass and ate the whole thing.

He was not stuffed, but his hunger pangs had been comfortably satiated, and he was weary. In fact, he was exhausted. This day had been different, unlike any he had known before. He was ready to bed down for the night.

That unusual instinct of direction that God had given to some of his wild creatures now took over. The little kitten pointed his course toward the thicket where he had found shelter and hurried along. In the absence of the crevice in the sandstone cliff, that thicket was the only security he knew.

Twice his attention was caught by squirrels searching for nuts on the ground, both times when he was very close. One time he was almost on top of a small gray squirrel before it saw him and hurried away, but he did not give chase.

The sun had been long gone behind the mountain when he reached the thicket. He crawled far back into the shelter and bedded down in the same clump of leaves he had used earlier in the day. Now, like he and his mother used to do on the ledge outside their den, he listened to the night come in.

First he heard the song of the wood thrush. Then, all was quiet. Those sacred moments of silence known as twilight time had come.

Later, the silence was broken by a great horned owl floating over the forest roof. The big owl perched in a giant red spruce only a dozen or so feet from the little kitten's shelter. The soft but resonant "Whoo-aWhoo-aWhoooo" set the stage for the other voices of the night.

The panther kitten curled up his soft bed of leaves and went to sleep while a katydid rasped out his harsh night song.

14

His sleep was disturbed only once during the night. That was when a pair of young bears fought over their kill somewhere on the side of the mountain. It wasn't particularly frightening, yet he would have felt a lot more secure if he had been bedded down in that crevice in the cliff which he had, up until today, known as home.

CHAPTER 3

The panther kitten awoke with the first light of day. Yet he did not crawl out of his snug leaf bed until the sun had warmed the chill air on the mountain top.

This was the panther kitten's second day of fending for himself, and his hungry stomach was calling for vigorous action. Now nature, in it's kind and gentle way, was now beginning to take over.

The young hunter moved with more speed, but that was coupled with greater caution. He was more alert to all that was taking place about him. He was again finding ways to place his feet so that his movements were almost without sound.

He was learning to read the sounds of the forest more carefully, and to filter through his nostrils with greater ease the various odors that came with each change of the air currents. Mother Nature was telling him which currents to fear and which to follow. It was a learning experience that would last, not only for months, but most surely for years.

The panther kitten now dropped about halfway down the slope. This gave him more forest floor to see by checking both above and below him. Soon, he saw two half-grown woodchucks playing about their den beneath a large rotting stump.

It was evident that directly stalking the woodchucks was not possible, not on the dry forest floor. He dropped back, cutting in a half circle until the stump was between himself and the game. Now he began to stalk. He knew that the slightest sound would alert the chucks and send them racing for their den.

When he reached the stump, he peeped around it. One of the chucks was off by itself nibbling on a plant. The kitten had learned from his mother that a moment's hesitation could mean the difference between food and famine. So he did not hesitate. He leaped, and his second bound landed him between the chuck and its den entrance.

The chuck was not intimidated. He was cut off, but he was a fighter. He came at his assailant, clicking his teeth and growling.

The panther kitten knew at once that he was in for a fight. He thought back to the chipmunk teeth he had encountered yesterday. These teeth looked much larger than the chipmunk's teeth, much more imposing. He had to avoid them.

When the chuck was close enough, the panther kitten leaped in and swatted him with a left forepaw that sent the woodchuck rolling. The kitten tried to get at the animal's throat before he could gain his feet, but the chuck was up and at him again, still aggressive, still pressing the fight.

A second, and then a third time, the panther kitten rolled the chuck, but was unable to get at the chuck's exposed throat. When he finally got hold of the chuck's throat, he gripped with all his strength and pushed down hard.

The chuck did not die easy. He tried to wiggle out from under his attacker and fought with all four feet. But the kitten did not release his hold until the body went limp. Only then did he drop the kill and back off.

The panther kitten had just fought his first real battle. His other two kills had been easy. Here, though, he had faced a capable and determined fighter. And he could now consider himself a winner. Although he had a little advantage in size over the chuck, they still had been rather well matched.

There was a lot of tough skin between him and the nourishment his hungry body was crying so loudly for. So he wasted no time, chewing away the tough skin to get at the sweet warm meat beneath it.

For the first time since he had left the den, his stomach was comfortably stuffed. He had spent the better part of an hour nibbling bits of meat off bones and skin. When he got up from his meal, all that was left of the chuck was the head, hide and leg bones.

Now, the little panther's desire was to put more miles between himself and the scene of disaster. He continued out the side of the mountain until it dropped off into a deep cross-draw, where a small creek meandered down its rock-strewn bed.

Although he was comfortably full, it was the panther's nature to constantly be on the alert for food. When he uncovered a crawfish, he munched on it. As he continued his search, a frog found its way into his stuffed maw.

He climbed onto a fallen log which formed a bridge across the creek, and he was able to cross the stream with dry feet. He now began the climb up the mountain on the far side of the creek. He was moving without apparent purpose, other than to distance himself from the bold hump where his dead mother lay.

As he meandered down the mountain, he noted a change in vegetation as he dropped away from the higher peaks. He found his way through a thicket of laurel. Coming out the other side, he surprised a covey of grouse feeding on the ground beneath a spangling oak. He could hear them scratching among the leaves and talking to each other well before he saw them. They were so near the color of the brown leaves about them that they were difficult to spot. None of the birds were close when his head first broke cover. So he came forward quietly, a slow step at a time, slinking down low.

He was fresh off of his first real win and was feeling great confidence in himself. He leaped among the birds. He struck one to the ground with a right forepaw. But the grouse was back up and beating the air with flailing wings before he could strike it down again. He had lost this one. It didn't bother him from the standpoint of hunger. He was still comfortably full, but after his first real win, he had suddenly become a sore loser.

He gave forth with a feeble squall and continued down the mountain slope, swinging back and forth, searching. The evening shadow of the western mountain was climbing up the slope.

Suddenly, the sun was gone. He didn't wonder why. Nor did he look up and see the dark clouds that had begun to roll in. But he was aware of the wind that had kicked up, blowing leaves and bits of dirt into his face.

He had just come onto a narrow little bench, when his attention was caught by a heavy scratching in the leaves. He recognized the sound at once. It was a flock of wild turkeys, chirping and gobbling, feeding as they travelled.

He had once watched his mother stalk such a flock. She had waited in her cover until the flock was near. Then she had leaped among them, striking down a big gobbler and a smaller hen. The hen had been able to get to her feet and went flopping away with the flock as they all took to the air. His mother had smashed the gobbler down with a second blow and had then crushed its head with her jaws.

They had waited until the dead turkey stopped flopping. Then his mother tore back the breast skin to expose the white muscle beneath. The kitten had never eaten white meat before. He thought it was very special.

These turkeys had caught his attention so completely that he failed to see that a storm was rolling in very fast. He flattened himself down beside a big oak tree and waited for the turkeys to advance toward him.

The flock of big birds continued past. They were all adults, no little ones. He looked at the long legs and the huge bodies, which frightened him a bit. Yet he remembered how the turkeys had gone down under the mallet-like blow of his mother's forepaw. As a big hen turkey passed near him, he made up his mind. The two turkeys had been easy game for his mother. Certainly, he could handle one. He lunged out, aiming for the broad back of the nearest hen.

The turkey immediately spotted him. She started to run, flapping her wings in an effort to get airborne. A wing brushed the panther kitten and almost knocked him away, but he had enough momentum to carry his strike through.

The kitten came down on the turkey's back, but the big hen did not sink down onto the ground, as when his mother came down on the big gobbler's back. This big bronze bird just kept running and flapping her wings.

By now the entire flock was airborne. And the kitten's big catch was staying right with them, only a tiny bit behind because of the weight she was carrying. Yet she was airborne like the rest of those huge winged critters.

The kitten was frightened. Nothing had gone as he had expected it to go. He was clinging to the sides of the turkey with his needle sharp claws, and she was squawking in pain.

The turkey turned its head and tried to peck him. But he just ducked a little farther back, still holding on desperately.

He wanted out of this frightening situation, but when he looked down, the earth was several feet below him. He did not want to fall, so he held on tight.

When they passed around a bend in the bench, the lead turkey landed. The others soon followed, and as his turkey's feet touched ground, the kitten abandoned ship.

The little panther hit the earth with a thud and rolled over several times before he was able to get on his feet. When he came to a stop he just stood there, watching as the flock raced away around the side of the mountain.

He hadn't been able to bring down one of those big birds, but he had learned another rough lesson. It would be a long time before he tackled another critter that much larger than himself. Still, he had hit the ground moving and had not gotten severely hurt. Maybe his feelings were hurt a little bit, but that would not slow him down. Sometime later, he decided, when he had grown a lot more, he would feast again on white turkey meat.

The flock was hardly out of sight when the little panther felt the first big rain drops on his back. Only then did he become aware that the storm was already upon him. It was right there with a bang, and he was out in the open.

He had never been outside his den in a storm such as this one promised to be. Many times he had watched the rain and lightning from the safety of his lair. There he had been safe and dry, and, in a way, had enjoyed the show.

He suddenly felt the need for shelter. Then a big flash of light appeared just up the mountain from him, followed shortly by an ear-splitting crash of thunder. This added new urgency to his mission.

Just under the crest of the mountain, on the other side of the bench where he had been ditched, was a series of broken cliff-like rock formations. Since his home had been within such a setting, he dashed toward it as fast as his little legs would carry him.

He searched frantically among the rocks until he found a deep cavity beneath a larger ledges. Without hesitation or thought of danger, he dived into the shelter, the rain splashing heavily on his back.

When he landed in the cavity, he found himself face to face with a big male raccoon. The animal let out a screech and bowed up his back until he looked twice his normal size. With his needle sharp teeth bared, he started toward the kitten.

The teeth in that big mouth looked quite impressive to a little panther who had not forgotten the first bite he had received. And that little mouth had been insignificant compared to the set of teeth now coming at him. The old boar coon growled fiercely.

The kitten beat a hasty retreat. Dashing back into the rain, he leaped down the hill with a great bound.

When he was certain that the coon was not following him, he came back up to the ledge and continued around the base of the rock formations, keeping an eye out behind him until he found another cavity. It wasn't as spacious as the one he had just given up, but it was dry, and there were no other critters in it to challenge him.

He shook the rain out of his eyes so he could get a good look about him. He thought he detected movement at the far end of the shelter. He blinked his eyes again, and took a second look. Yes, there was something there, but it looked smaller than himself. He was afraid of animals larger than himself, not smaller ones.

Then the little black animal in the far end of the cavity turned to face him. He saw the two white stripes down the critter's back.

Whoa, a skunk!

He wanted no association with that smelly critter. He was almost ready to hit the rain again when he realized that the skunk had made no move toward him.

His first encounter with one of those stinking characters had been when he was still a tiny spotted kitten. His mother had cleverly avoided the skunk, but the kitten had attempted to make friends with it.

The skunk had misunderstood the kitten's intentions and favored him with a heavy dose of the smelly chemical he was equipped with and so famous for using.

The kitten had spent weeks so stinking that he could hardly stand himself. He had bathed in the creek, rolled in the dirt, and scrubbed himself on rocks and trees, but the stench had lingered with him for quite a long time. Even his mother had tried to avoid him as much as possible.

Very soon, when neither the panther nor the skunk made any move toward the other, they apparently decided that they were no threat to each other. Each of them seemed to be satisfied to hold to his end of the cavity.

The skunk turned his attention back to the storm. He was eagerly awaiting its end. Since he sustained himself principally on insects and grubs, he knew that the rain would bring such critters up from among the wet leaves and rain-soaked ground. That would make hunting easy.

The storm was fierce. Distant peals of thunder came closer and closer until they seemed to the little panther to be right on the mountain top above his head. In fact, they were -- right there on top of his mountain, and all the other mountains around, -- spitting fire and rumbling in an almost constant roar.

The panther kitten crowded back against the rear wall of the cavity as blinding flashes of light came one after the other. Great waves of rain pounded the mountain side. The howling wind sent the rain spraying all the way back to where the little panther crouched, trying to keep dry.

When the storm had passed, he sat tight in his temporary home. It was nearing nightfall, and he was still gripped by fear from the fierceness of the storm. He felt secure where he was. At least he had a good stone roof over his head. And his neighbor had moved on to complete his night's hunt.

Again, he listened to the night come in. There was a deeper chill in the air tonight, possibly caused by the storm, so he curled up in a ball and went to sleep, even before the wood thrushes ceased their chorus.

Only once during the night was his rest disturbed, when a wildcat screamed in the valley far below him. It was answered by another wildcat on the crest of the mountain directly above him. That wildcat sounded so near that it sent little tingles of fear through his body.

For the first time since he lost his mother, he felt real fear invading his entire being. He felt helpless against such creatures as these wildcats without his mother at his side. He moved back in the cavity until he was tight against the rock wall and prepared to defend himself.

His fear of wildcats dated back to the time he had watched a bout between his mother and a big tom wildcat. The mother panther had taken the wildcat's kill away from him and he didn't concede easy. Although much smaller than his opponent, the wildcat had dared to spar with her, screaming and spitting as he leaped nimbly away from her many charges.

The kitten had been so frightened by that encounter, that he had hidden behind a rock until the wildcat finally gave up and went away, still grumbling. That was the first and only animal he had seen challenge his mother, and it remained fixed in his young mind. He had held a particular fear of wildcats since that encounter.

Before he could sleep again, a gray fox squalled somewhere on the slope below him, but that call fostered little fear in the young panther. It was a gentle voice when compared to the scream of a wildcat

Later in the night, when a barred owl decided to add his querulous call to the voices of the deep dark, Saber was tempted to go to the entrance of his assumed home and try a scream of his own. Yet fear from the wildcat calls kept him back.

CHAPTER 4

The next morning, the panther kitten came out from beneath the rock ledge. Another day of his new life was now before him, and he felt eager to be about it.

The kitten's world was now expanding rapidly. He was much more alert to the new sounds, the new creatures and the new scents that kept him in touch with the world around him.

Before he climbed up to the crest of the mountain, he listened to the chirping of a flock of migrating wood warblers, and the honking of a flock of wild geese far up in the sky. Like the warblers, they too were heading south. A fox squirrel scolded from a safe spot well up in a tree. A chipmunk chipped loudly as he scampered for the safety of his den.

Before the kitten had reached the mountain crest, he was stopped abruptly by the a sharp buzzing. He froze in place, until his keen eyes detected a coiled rattler in the trail.

Though he had never seen a snake before, Mother Nature was telling him to stay clear of that creature. He backed away cautiously, and circled wide, picking his steps carefully, before he came back onto the trail he had been following.

One he had reached the mountain top, he could see nothing but other mountains in every direction. In fact, his whole world was made up of hills and valleys, deep draws, little creeks and small branches. He dropped off on the far side of the mountain he had just come up. That would carry him to the southeast. Why fate was leading the panther kitten on such a course he could not understand, nor did he try to.

The image of the big cat who had always brought him food popped into the kitten's mind whenever hunger pangs knifed at his middle the hardest, and now was one of those times. By the time he reached the valley, the sun was almost straight up and he had found nothing larger than a katydid to munch on. His stomach continued crying loudly for something edible. How great it would be if that big head could just drop a warm, juicy chunk of red meat right down in front of him now.

He was following a fair-sized creek when he smelled meat of some kind. It wasn't strong but it was there, somewhere near. He began to search for the source of that odor. Abruptly the scent grew weaker, so he turned back and checked both sides of the trail again.

The strong odor indicated something edible, and he was determined to find it. His hungry innards told him to keep looking. Now the odor grew weaker, so once more he turned back on the trail.

He had been confining his search to the ground. It hadn't occurred to him to look up, until he saw a bird flit across the trail and light on something. A piece of meat hung on a string from a tree limb above the path.

The meat was too high for him to reach. He had no idea how the meat had gotten up there, but his hungry stomach was telling him to get it.

He moved closer. He stood up and reached as high as possible, but the meat was still too high. He leaped up, tried to grasp the meat with his right front foot, but missed and dropped back.

As he landed he heard a loud snap and something grabbed his left rear foot. He sprang away but the thing that had clamped onto his foot held fast. He landed on his side and came up fighting.

After a brief struggle, he paused to study what was holding him. He saw the long spring of a steel trap, and iron jaws holding his foot.

He tried again and again to jerk his foot free but to no avail. The trap was secured to the ground by a chain attached to a peg in the ground. He bit the trap and fought it with his free feet, but still it held. He soon realized that pulling on his foot was causing additional pain. So he lay down and waited.

The kitten had no way of knowing that what held him was a trap set for mink. Nor could he know that tomorrow morning the trapper would make his rounds looking for skins to place on stretching frames in his fur shed. So he could not know what fate awaited him unless he could somehow be rescued.

PART II
CHAPTER 5

It has often been said that disaster loves company and that it usually comes in bunches. So it was, that in the little community of Cave Creek Valley, disaster was to strike on August 25, the same day that it had torn apart a panther family some fifty miles deep in the mythical wilds of the Monongahela.

It had now been twelve years since the trap door was opened and Old Crooked Toe, the panther who had been, and still was a legend in the valley, was released back to his wilderness home. On the day following Old Crooked Toe's release, Kennie Reeves and Katie Bonner had exchanged vows in the little log church at the south end of the valley.

There had been many changes in the valley in those twelve years, mostly in the farming methods. The biggest change was that the teams of work horses had been replaced by gasoline powered tractors. All, that is, except faithful old Prince. Although Kennie Reeves had also gone to a tractor to turn the sod and pull the harvesting equipment, he and Prince still had little chores they enjoyed doing together.

Although most of the gardeners now tilled their gardens with gasoline power, Prince still pulled the cultivator between the rows in Kennie's garden.

That normally consumed close to a half hour every week.

One of the reasons Prince enjoyed those occasions could have been that, when the task was over, there would be a double handful of chopped apples in his feed box when the harness was removed.

Kennie and Prince also pulled the cultivator through Kennie's mother's garden. And again that culminated in a generous feast of chopped apples when the task was completed.

There had been other changes in the valley. Jerry Beeler had lost his wife, and his brother Tom had come down with crippling arthritis. Katie Reeves had lost her father. She and Kennie had bought a farm adjoining Kennie's mother, so they could be close to Nancy.

Cory and Agnes Long had suffered a very bad car wreck. Cory had not been hurt seriously, but Agnes was broken up terribly.

For weeks Agnes lay in a coma in the hospital with no sign of improvement. Finally, the doctor and the special nurse caring for Agnes had met with the family. The time had come to remove all life-support.

Regrettably, the family consented. Then, much to everyone's amazement, Agnes began to recover immediately. Although still crippled in some ways, she was able to go home in less than a week. The doctor and nurse, who had worked so diligently over Agnes, declared it nothing short of a miracle. Medical science had given up. God had taken over. Once again, Agnes Long was that stalwart of faith where residents of the valley came to seek help with their prayer needs.

THE LOST BOY

A few families had left the valley, but there had been a half dozen new arrivals. The valley had remained a close knit community.

So it was that Kennie and Katie Reeves were celebrating their twelfth wedding anniversary on this twenty fifth day of August. Yet there were other events to celebrate.

It was on the day of their first anniversary that Kennie and Katie had welcomed their first child. Katie had gone into her mother's Italian ancestry and come up with the name Antonio, which she had changed to the English spelling of Anthony. So Anthony J. Reeves was celebrating his eleventh birthday.

Again that was not all.

It just happened that ancient old Pete Higgins was born on the twenty fifth day of August, and on this special day he was celebrating his 90th birthday. Since Pete's friend Dudley Newberry had passed on, Pete was the oldest resident in the valley. So, with Kennie and Katie's friends, Anthony's little friends, and Pete's crowd, it had begun to look more like a community gathering.

The gala affair was held over on the back side of Pete's place under the great maple trees that everyone in the valley so adored. And there was food. Great baskets of food, all spread out on the brightly colored maple leaves carpeting the forest floor.

After everyone was comfortably stuffed, there had been presents. Many presents for Grandpa Pete, as everyone in the valley had come to call him. Presents from many in the valley who still remembered that Pete had been the one everyone in the Valley had called on for help, before his wreck. Presents for Grandpa Pete from Pam and Becky Lee and their many friends and family members. For, after these many years, with Becky a senior in high school, they still had not forgotten that Pete's crippled condition had been brought on by saving Becky from a speeding car when she was only a toddler.

For the Reeves family there had been gifts from a few special friends. Kennie and Katie had exchanged gifts, then there was a special gift for Anthony.

Since he was an aspiring photographer, Anthony was doubly elated when he opened his gift and found a professional camera, with a bag of film and a carrying case with a belt for strapping it over his shoulder. He wasted no time getting the camera loaded and in action.

Shortly thereafter, Pam Lee decided to take a group of the young folks on a walk through the mountain side. Of course, Anthony was eager to join the walk. It possibly would afford an opportunity to get some wildlife pictures.

Pam led the group about a third of the way up the mountain face, then turned south, winding into the little valleys, then around the hump of the next ridge, with Anthony searching constantly for an opportunity to snap a picture.

Abruptly Anthony's attention was caught by a migrating flock of wood warblers. The shy little birds kept flitting away, until he broke away from the group and followed the flock up the mountain side. He saw a special little yellow warbler that he wanted to get a picture of. But the little bird kept too far away to get anything like a close-up shot.

The warblers kept Anthony interested until they reached the mountain top, then they flew away. He was ready to drop back down the mountain and join the party when he noticed a spot of bright red down the back slope of the mountain. There was some jet black mixed with the red.

Anthony knew at once that it was a scarlet tanager. What a great shot that would make to start his wildlife collection. So off he went again -- down the back side of the Mountain.

Now this handsome little jewel of the bird world was even shyer than the warblers. Getting close enough for a shot proved difficult, if not impossible. Yet Anthony kept following. Before he realized what was happening, the bird had led him all the way down to the foot of the mountain. Then it led him a hundred yards or so to the north. There, it flew up into the tree tops and vanished.

In the process of following the tanager, Anthony had crossed and re-crossed the little brook that separated Sugar Maple Mountain from the edge of the Monongahela. So, when he decided it was time to climb back up the mountain and head home, he wasn't sure which side of the brook he was on.

For some minutes Anthony studied the mountains on either side of the brook. Neither one looked familiar because the bird had led him so far. He had a faint feeling that he might be confused, maybe even lost. But it lasted only for brief seconds.

He would follow his own good judgment. That was what his father had told him to do when they walked Sugar Maple Mountain or in the east hills.

CHAPTER 6

L ike most persons who are lost, Anthony started out in the opposite direction from which he should have been going. Then, he climbed the wrong mountain.

It seemed a little steeper than he had expected, but then the bird had led him some distance to the north. He figured that he would go down the other side of the mountain and discover that he was on the north end of Cave Creek Valley. So, when he reached the top of the mountain, down he went.

The terrain was becoming more rugged. There was fallen timber, resembling land that had never been cut over. That fostered more undergrowth, so heavy in places that he had to find his way around some of the thickets. He paused, looking back up to where he had come from.

For a moment Anthony considered climbing back up the mountain and trying to retrace his steps. But then he decided to continue on down the slope he was on. Maybe he would see something familiar. He and his father had wandered some in the wilds of the Monongahela, so he might come to an area they had traversed before. Yes, just maybe.

But when he got to the foot of the mountain, there was nothing, not a landmark of any kind.

THE LOST BOY

Finally, Anthony had to admit to himself that he was lost. He had no idea which way to turn. So he tried to remember all the things his Dad had told him to do if ever he got lost.

One of the first things to do when lost in the wilderness was to get a walking stick. His Dad had said, "A mountain man without a sturdy walking stick is really handicapped."

He folded his camera and placed it in the case on his side. He dug his knife out of his pocket, and soon found a small sapling that he cut off to make a walking stick.

Another thing he remembered was to find a shelter before night set in, and get as comfortable as possible. This made him suddenly aware that evening shadows were beginning to darken the forest about him.

Down the little valley he was now in, he could see a hard packed game trail. That was something he wanted to avoid. So he began climbing up the next mountain, searching for a place to hide for the night.

About half way up the side of the mountain he came upon a rock ledge. He searched along the ledge until he found two rock formations about two feet apart that ran into the hill.

Night was now coming in fast, so Anthony searched frantically until he found sticks and brush enough to make a covering over the top of the two rocks. With this temporary roof over it, the cavity was not high enough for him to stand, but when he scooted back into it he was able to get himself fairly comfortable sitting up. And if he wanted to lay down, of course, it was deep enough for that also.

Anthony felt that he was on the safest part of the mountain. Most wildlife would either be following the top of the ridge above him, or padding along the game trail down at the foot of the hill. Still, and for the first time since he realized he was lost, he began to feel real fear.

He was alone. He didn't know where he was, only that he was somewhere in the vast wilderness of the Monongahela National Forest.

Darkness swept down the steep slopes about Anthony very fast. It was as though night was eager to envelop the world about the lost boy with an aura of mystique and mystery, as he huddled in his hastily prepared shelter.

A few song birds gave their final trills just before that sacred hour of silence known as twilight. Though Anthony had always enjoyed the restful quiet of the twilight hour, this time, the silence seemed oppressive. Then, the katydids began their song. Yet even they seemed few and far between.

Anthony realized that he must think positive. He also realized that he was hungry. He usually carried a candy bar or two with him. He felt in his pocket. Yes, there was one, only one. He took it out and unwrapped one half, which he ate. He was about to put the other half in his pocket when he changed his mind. Tomorrow would have to provide for itself. He ate the other half.

He was getting fairly well settled into his night shelter when a coyote yapped from the top of the mountain, almost directly over him. It sounded so very close.

That was unsettling. He had heard coyotes off in the eastern hills many times. But this was different. There, he had then been safe in his home. He was not home now. And he had no idea how far he was from the security of home. He only knew that he was somewhere in the vast wilds of the Monongahela, and he was lost. Hopelessly lost.

The yapping coyote moved away. Anthony was just getting settled down in his shelter again when he heard a shuffling in the leaves. It sounded very near his shelter. And it was coming closer -- much closer and very fast.

He got a good grip on his walking stick and braced himself against the back wall of his enclosure.

Anthony was sitting up, so when a small black animal paused to look into his shelter, he could see it's back. And there were those two white stripes down it's back, plainly visible, even in the darkness -- one on either side. A skunk.

He wanted no argument with that animal, especially when it was so close and he was in such cramped quarters. He eased his grip on the walking stick and tried to sit very still.

Then, when he thought the skunk had lingered too long, he had an idea -- bark like a dog. He tried it.

Whether the barking had any effect on the skunk, Anthony wasn't sure. The little rascal didn't change his pace. He just kept meandering along at his normal speed until the sound of rustling leaves around the side of the hill was no longer audible.

When Anthony got settled in his new quarters, his mind turned back to the happenings of the day. He wasn't sure just how many hills he had gone up and come down. But he knew he was very tired, particularly in his legs. He saw the silvery rim of a new moon appear over the mountain top across from him. A red fox barked from the ridge-top above and he fell asleep, trying to determine just what he should do when day came again.

Somewhere, far in the night, a search party cruised up the valley below Anthony, frequently calling his name. But he was so sound asleep that he never heard them.

CHAPTER 7

Day two of Anthony's ordeal came early. The shadows of night were still clinging stubbornly to the slope of the mountain about him when Anthony was awakened by a loud screeching. Soon he heard a raucous chattering outside his shelter.

Half in fear, half in curiosity, Anthony peered out of his shelter. What he saw sent his hands hurrying to get his camera out of the case.

In a great gnarled oak on the slope below him, a gray squirrel and a screech owl were fighting over a hole in the side of the tree. The squirrel was attempting to take over the little owl's home in the oak, and the homeowner wasn't going away peacefully.

Right then, the squirrel was winning. He was clinging to the side of the tree just ready to enter the hole, and the owl was on a nearby limb screeching loudly.

Anthony got his first picture just as the squirrel poked his head in the hole. Then, the owl flew down and struck the squirrel on the back. The squirrel whirled his head around to give fight, but the owl was already perched on a nearby limb, voicing his protest loudly.

Again the squirrel tried to enter the hole, and again he got hit. Apparently, the little owl's needle sharp talons were doing what he intended them to do.

For, when the squirrel got hit a third time, he gave up and scooted down the tree, running away in the leaves.

The owl flew to the hole, screeched loudly, then disappeared into his reclaimed home.

Anthony folded his camera and placed it securely in its case. Maybe it wasn't so bad being lost in the wilderness after all. Yet, when his empty stomach cried out loudly for food, maybe it wasn't so good either.

Now awake, Anthony decided to climb to the mountain top above his shelter. Maybe from that vantage point he could see something that would help him get his bearings.

He was following a small game trail when he heard the buzzing of a snake's rattles. He jumped back and stood very still until he could see the coiled rattler in the path. Moving very slowly, he stepped from the trail and circled wide.

When he came back to the trail, he used his walking stick to part the low brush before stepping into the beaten path. Then he heard a second rattler.

Two snakes, so close together! Certainly he was in rattlesnake territory. He had heard that rattlesnakes often frequented huckleberry country. That reminded him of his need for food -- Something to quell the hunger pangs that were increasing as he climbed the steep hillside. He began looking for huckleberry bushes. Even though back home the huckleberries had come and gone, at this high altitude, the berries might ripen later. And he found them -- Deep blue berries on a patch of low bushes.

The few berries left were rather shrunken, but they were edible. By scouring the entire patch he was able to gather a handful of berries. He went looking for more and found a second patch. These berries, even higher up the ridge, were fuller. Again he searched the entire patch and was able to gather more. It wasn't a big breakfast, but it helped.

When he finally reached the mountain top, he could see nothing but more mountains, with not a clue where he was. Not a familiar landmark, nothing but hills and valleys, and they all looked alike.

He had been thirsty ever since eating the candy bar last night. It was time to find water. He decided to drop over on the other side of the mountain. He thought he would probably have to go down some distance to find a spring.

He was right. About half way down the slope he found a spring coming out from beneath a rock ledge. He was surprised at the volume of water. It was gushing down the steep slope to spread out in a little swale. He saw a clump of shrubs that were greener than the rest of the forest about them.

After he drank his fill he decided to check out that clump of shrubbery that seemed so different from those about them.

He had to circle a rock ledge to get to the little trees. Much to his surprise, when he finally reached them, he found a thicket of wild plumbs.

The squirrels and birds had done a job on the fruit of the bushes, but there were still some plumbs on the outer limbs that the critters had not gotten to.

Using his walking stick, Anthony was able to knock a number of plumbs to the ground. He gathered a handful and sat on a rock. He ate several plumbs, chewing away the fruit and spitting out the seeds. Then he went back to gather some to carry with him.

He had his extra camera film in a plastic bag. He emptied the film into his pocket and filled the bag with plumbs. The full bag would not fit into his pocket so he opened his shirt, put the bag inside and buttoned the shirt again.

The day was going well for the lost boy. At least, his hunger pangs had been fairly well satisfied. He had a small store of food tucked away in his shirt, and the day was still young.

Now if he could only hone in on a course toward home, maybe only a starting point, and a direction to follow. If so, he could be home before nightfall.

The question was, which way to turn? Below him was a valley with a small meandering stream. There was also a much used game trail. He was about to go on down to the trail when he heard something.

Abruptly a small deer ran down the trail with a coyote close on its heels.

Anthony ducked in behind a clump of shrubs until the deer and the coyote were out of sight. That trail was too busy for comfort, so he turned back up the slope.

He ate a couple more plumbs, then climbed back up the mountain. He was now under a large grove of oaks that were still holding tight to their leaves. That was when he heard the helicopter.

He tried to see the aircraft, but the leaf cover above him was too thick. As it came closer, he could see it flying close to the tree tops. It flew to the end of the mountain, then dropped over the side and flew up the valley where he had just seen the deer and coyote. He wondered what a helicopter could be doing this far away from its base.

Anthony had heard tales about people lost in the wilderness surviving by eating acorns. While he was under all these oaks he decided to see just how the acorns would taste.

He searched among the leaves of two different trees and found an acorn from each tree. He got out his knife, opened one up and nibbled a bit. It was bitter and a little astringent. Certainly it would not make a pleasant meal. He tried the other acorn. It was milder but not something one would relish, except in an emergency.

Anthony stood there beneath the great oak trees deep in thought. He was beginning to think like an adult. He had accepted the fact that he was hopelessly lost. He had expected search teams to find him long before now. He had no way of knowing that one team had passed him by when he was sound asleep, calling his name loudly.

Another thought struck Anthony as he paused under those towering trees. That helicopter, it was looking for him. It had not been able to see him through the heavy foliage. It would not be coming back this way. He had seen it cruise down the mountain, swing over and fly low up the next valley. Then it had disappeared over the next mountain. It was gone. It would not be coming back.

Not today. Maybe never.

For a moment Anthony was overcome by utter despair, but it lasted only briefly. He slapped himself sharp on the cheek with an open hand.

"You've got to think positive," he told himself. "Remember the story Dad told about the terrible night and how the old panther had saved him."

Maybe that old panther was still somewhere in the Monongahela. Maybe he would save him and he would have a great story to tell that would match the one his Dad had told so many times.

Now he was thinking positive. He knew he could survive in the wilderness. He opened another one of the acorns and ate about half of it. He then stooped down, searched among the leaves, and filled a hip pocket with the milder acorns. They would be there in case of dire emergency.

He suddenly wanted to be away from this heavy growth of trees. They had foiled his rescue. Probably the helicopter would never come this way again. But if it did, he didn't want to be under these trees.

He dropped over the mountain and found his way down into the next valley. The only thing he encountered on the way down was a black snake. The snake went one way and he went the other. Each seemed satisfied with their individual decisions.

In this valley, he also found a spring and drank his fill. Then he began climbing the opposite slope. About half way up he came upon a giant hickory. It must have had a bumper crop of nuts, for there were squirrels in the tree, many squirrels. There was a big fox squirrel and two grays searching for nuts in the leaves beneath it. He reasoned that if he had a gun and some matches he would have roast squirrel for dinner. But he had neither.

As Anthony watched the squirrels, a red tailed hawk screamed. That caught the attention of the squirrels. The fox squirrel and one gray headed for the hickory. The hawk was already in a steep dive. The other gray, farther out, tried to reach an outlying tree, but he never made it. Not by at least a dozen feet. The hawk swooped down, caught the squirrel in his talons, and swooped back up through the trees. It was a scene rarely witnessed. Anthony wished he could have gotten a picture, but it had all happened in a flash. There was not even time to think, much less to get his camera out of the case and focus. He figured that the hawk was either feeding a nest of babies or that he would have a full meal for dinner.

He climbed to the top of this mountain, but could see no landmarks that helped him. Again here was nothing but more mountains. He followed the ridge until it dropped sharply off into a deep valley, where he found a much larger creek than he had seen so far. There was no creek that size near Sugar Maple Mountain, so he must have travelled too far north.

The day was now spent. Already the sun was sinking behind the high ground to the west. It was time to start looking for shelter.

The creek had taken him around a bluff and turned him back to the north. Now he climbed the mountain about half way and looked for a place to spend the night. He found nothing to his liking, so he went down into the next draw and started around the next incline.

Out ahead he saw some rock ledges. Possibly that was his best bet. About half way around, he saw a big oak tree with a hole in its side. It looked much like the tree where the owl and squirrel had fought that morning.

He wondered about two trees looking so much alike. Then he looked above where he was standing. About seven feet up was the shelter he had used last night. He had spent the full day traveling in a great circle.

How discouraging. He was no closer home than he had been when he started the day. Then he thought again. At least he was no farther from home. Yet, with this situation, coupled with missing the helicopter, it had not been a good day. But he did have a good place to spend the night. Tomorrow would be a better day. He felt sure of that.

Anthony scooted back into his shelter. He felt a little safer tonight, that is until he heard a panther scream. It was a call like none he had ever heard before. It came shortly after night was full, before the rim of a moon peeped over the eastern mountains, so everything about his shelter was in total darkness.

The call had been a bit unnerving, even though he knew it had come from a mountain top some distance away. Still, he would be safe for the night, or would he? Visions of coyotes, bears, and wildcats flooded his mind. He recalled stories about the famous panther known as Old Crooked Toe. Could this panther he had just heard be the same one? If it was, he would have to be very old.

He found himself hoping that the animal, which had voiced his presence so loudly, was Old Crooked Toe in person. Maybe, just maybe, that legendary old creature that he had heard so many stories about would save him.

And why not? It had once saved his Dad. If such a thing did happen, what a great story he would have to tell when, and if he got home! He admonished himself for that 'and if.' He needed to think positive. He would get home, the only question was, when.

Anthony fell asleep, building plots in his mind about how Old Crooked Toe was going to come to his rescue. Needless to say, his sleep was filled with dreams about panthers, but they were not all good. Maybe half, maybe less.

CHAPTER 8

Anthony was so tired from his hike the day before, that he did not awaken until there was a violent commotion directly above him. A broad winged hawk, chased by a flock of crows, had sought haven in a towering oak near Anthony's sleeping quarters. The raucous calls of the crows, as they dived at the hawk, set the forest ringing and sent squirrels and other creatures scrambling for shelter.

Anthony crawled out of his hole in the rocks with hopes of getting a picture. But before he could get his camera out of the case the hawk saw him and flew away, followed by the full host of his pursuers.

Oh well, it would have been too far away to get a good picture. So what? He found a rock to perch and ate four of his plumbs while he made his plans for the day.

Today, Anthony determined, he would not travel in another circle. He could never get home that way. He would wait for the sun to come up. Then, using it as a guide, he would travel south for the better part of the morning. After that he would try to hold an easterly course.

When he had first gotten lost, he had travelled away from the western side of Sugar Maple Mountain, to the northwest. So, to get back, he would have to go south and east.

Everything went well for a while, then he had to climb over the ridge of the next mountain to keep his course. That carried him down into a deep valley which turned him to the east. Now he found himself following the low lands, the valleys.

Up a deep draw he saw something that looked like it might have once been a log cabin. Maybe it was a trapper's cabin, or possibly a residence from the time before the Federal Government bought up the land and added it to the National Forest. He decided to check.

Sure enough, it had been a residence at some time, but now it was crumbling down into Mother Earth again. In typical mountain fashion, it had been built close to a great spring where water was still gushing. And there had been a tiny orchard and a garden spot, now heavily overgrown with sprouts and briar vines. Two apple trees, in what had been the orchard, had survived the years but they were overrun with wild foliage. And where there had been a garden there was now a jumble of young, very thick growth, bramble almost impenetrable. Yet he felt a need to get to those apple trees.

Anthony beat his way back to the apple trees with his walking stick. It wasn't easy but he made it, with a bruise or two and a number of briar scratches.

One tree had apparently been a summer apple, for there was no fruit on it. In fact, it had already begun to drop it's leaves. But the other tree was a winter apple and he was able to find two apples on the outer limbs that the squirrels had missed. He knocked them off with his walking stick. This was an unusual find here deep in the wilderness.

He fondled the apples for a minute, then ate one and put the other in his pocket. But he was still hungry, very hungry. He found his way back out of the thicket and dug the second apple out of his pocket.

Anthony looked around for a place to sit and enjoy his apple, when he spotted an unusual formation. It looked like someone had started to build a dirt pyramid, but had stopped halfway through. It looked soft and inviting, so he parked himself on it and sailed into the second apple. He took his time enjoying it.

By the time he finished the apple he had the sensation that something was crawling up his legs. He lifted his pants legs and discovered that his legs were covered with tiny light red ants. He had been sitting on an ant hill.

Anthony jumped up, grabbed his walking stick and climbed up the slope to the trunk of a fallen tree. He sat there for several minutes trying to rid himself of ants, but it wasn't easy. By now they were on his arms, neck and some were on his cheeks.

Anthony had to laugh at himself when he looked around to see that no one was watching before he slipped off his pants, then his briefs and finally his shirt.

He used his shirt to beat the ants off of his body, then he vigorously shook out all of his clothes before he put them back on. Still, a few of the tiny creatures annoyed him as he worked his way back to the creek.

While he had stopped by the log cabin, clouds had crawled in and shut out the sun. But he knew his general course because of the creek he was following.

Within minutes the wind got up, the clouds grew darker and he could hear distant thunder. A big storm was coming his way. He needed to find shelter, maybe fast. A leaf covered shelter like the one he had used for the last two nights would not do. He needed some type of solid cover over his head.

He had heard stories about early pioneers finding shelter in giant hollow sycamore trees. Such trees frequently grew close to water and he was following a fair sized stream. He searched along the creek bank as he went. He found two large sycamores, but neither one was hollow.

The thunder was growing closer, following flashes of lightning that streaked across the sky, when he came to a third large sycamore. It was hollowed out sufficiently for him to get in. As great raindrops began to pepper him, he dove for the entrance.

Anthony was about halfway in the opening when something streaked by him so close that wing feathers stroked the side of his face. He turned his head in time to see a grouse flying away. The bird apparently had decided that two was a crowd and had given up it's shelter willingly.

The storm came in fast. Within minutes the rain was falling in great sheets. Peals of thunder almost overlapped each other. Lightning played among the trees atop the surrounding mountains. And in the bole of the great sycamore, as Anthony listened to the ferocity of the storm, he thanked God for his dry shelter. Without it he would have been soaked in seconds.

The rain was falling so hard a stream of water had formed, flowing down the center of the trail. A sudden flash of lightning revealed an animal loping up the trail. A second flash showed that it was a wildcat, and that it was coming closer very fast.

Anthony figured the cat was looking for shelter so he grabbed his walking stick with both hands. Possibly the animal knew about the hollow tree and was heading his way. In fact, that was where the big creature was headed.

As the cat poked his head in the entrance to the hollow, Anthony struck him as hard as he could wield his walking stick.

The wildcat squalled and jumped back. But he wanted in that shelter. He wasn't ready to give up. So he poked his head in a second time, and again Anthony was ready for him.

The cat drew back and hesitated. Anthony leaned close to the entrance and struck him a full body blow. That proved enough. With a final squall the cat started loping on up the trail.

Anthony had won his first battle. But he had also learned something.

He understood now what his Dad meant when he said, "A woodsman without a good 'sturdy' walking stick was handicapped."

This stick was too light. That last blow should have knocked the cat completely across the trail, but it didn't. The first thing tomorrow he would do something about that.

When the storm had passed, Anthony came out to look around. Little rivulets of water flowed swiftly down the ravine into the stream. And the size of the stream seemed to have almost doubled.

Anthony drank fresh rainwater from the flowing stream. Darkness was not far off, and he knew he would never find better shelter. So he crawled back into the sycamore, ate the last of his plumbs, and settled in for the night.

There were the normal night sounds, but nothing that disturbed Anthony. He had no trouble going to sleep when darkness settled over the forest.

Was he beginning to accept living in the wilderness as a way of life? No. Not at all. He was simply learning to accept what he could not change. Tomorrow he would try again. Yes, tomorrow would be a new day, a new start.

Sometime far into the night Anthony was awakened by the yapping of a whole bevy of coyotes. They sounded near. Apparently, they had made a kill on top of the ridge and were fighting over the carcass. He got a good grip on his walking stick and crouched back in the hollow of the tree.

While he huddled there, trembling with fear, he thought he heard his name called. He poked his head out of the hollow tree and listened intently. Then, some five, maybe even ten minutes later he heard his name again, faint and far away. He had felt all along that there were search parties looking for him both day and night. Now he was certain they were out there.

He wanted to come out of his tree house and shout an answer, but fear of alerting the coyotes to his location kept him silent.

Later in the night, after the din from the coyotes had gone away, he came out of his shelter and screamed a number of times. But of course, the search party had by then moved away, and he got no answer.

It was another setback. Antony was filled with gloom as he crawled back into the hollow of the sycamore. He could not know about the close call that first night, but he did know about missing the helicopter. It took a while for him to get back to sleep. When he did, he had troubling dreams about missed opportunities

CHAPTER 9

The next day four came before Anthony was ready for it. Some previous animal resident had carried a lot of leaves into the hollow of the sycamore and he was snuggled down in them. He had pulled his cap down over his exposed ear and turned his collar up around his neck. So he was both warm and comfortable when the usual forest noises woke him.

Three days of climbing up and down mountains was behind him. That, and the lack of sufficient food, was beginning to tell on him. He knew he would not find a better place to rest, so rest he did, right there in the security of his home in the hollow sycamore.

When Anthony finally came out of his wilderness lair, the bright sunshine had already dropped about halfway down the face of the mountain. He stretched and yawned big. He realized that was the first time he had done so since he had become lost.

Now, the first and most pressing thing to do was to find something to eat. Food was the first priority, and the next would be to find a better walking stick. He must not put that off. That could well have been a coyote wanting into his shelter last night, or maybe a more aggressive wildcat. Not a bear or panther, he hoped, as he crawled out into the brilliance of a new day, a day that could well find him on his way home. A search party had come close last night, where would they be today?-- Or, would he miss them, like he had missed the helicopter? He hoped not again.

First he had to find some food. His stomach would not let him forget that, so he racked his mind, thinking of all the things he had heard about wild foods. He would have to find something edible that would be readily available, and could be consumed without cooking.

There was one fruit he knew of in the forest, and it ripened in the fall. That was the paw-paw. He knew folks who had gathered them. Wilderness men called them mountain bananas. He had once tasted one. It wasn't an exciting fruit, but it was edible.

He sat on a rock, thinking of what people had said about finding them. He remembered one person saying he had found some in a creek shallow.

What was a creek shallow? Possibly it was just the man's expression. Maybe he had referred to the wide bit of level land that forms wherever a branch coming out of the mountains joins a creek.

He had been following a creek when the storm struck. He decided to return to the creek and follow it, keeping his eyes open for anything that might be called a "creek shallow." If he saw something that looked hopeful on the other side of the creek he would simply wade across and check.

He knew there were other edible plants in the woods. He searched his memory, but he could not think of any others. Then he remembered one, toothwort. It had a small edible bulb deep within it. Some people called it crow's foot because of the shape of the leaf. But he hadn't seen any crow's foot in his travels. There were several plants that he and his father had gathered for wild greens. But greens had to be cooked, so they were out.

He began his daily walk, checking his surroundings carefully for signs of foodstuff. He soon came across some areas of level land that might be called shallows. They occurred anywhere that two facing ridges butted down to the creek bottom. He checked them all. One, two, three. Nothing.

On the fourth level, he sighted a bush well away from the path with yellow spots on it. That was encouraging. His step quickened. As he approached the plant, he could see that it was another blank. The bush proved to be a small clump of hickory sprouts with some of the leaves turning yellow.

His search didn't look encouraging. But he wasn't giving up. The fifth level that he came upon was no more than a couple hundred feet up the creek. There he found a broad little valley set back between two hills. He turned up the depression with high hopes.

He was about a hundred feet into the valley when he saw a clump of large bushes or small trees that looked different from the other shrubs around them. His step quickened again.

Soon he was able to make out some bits of yellow. By the time he reached that strange clump of trees, he was running. And there they were — Paw-paws, mountain bananas. The bushes were loaded!

Anthony stood there for a moment just admiring the beautiful yellow fruit. Something had been eating on them, but there were plenty left for him. He gathered a double handful of paw-paws, found a rock to sit on, and sailed into them. Were they delicious? Maybe not to a well fed individual. But to a half-starved lost boy, they were fantastically delicious.

When he had eaten about half of the handful, he paused. He didn't want to make himself sick. Here he was, alone, away from home, far away from a doctor. He had to think for himself. And he was beginning to learn how. He was learning to think like an adult.

He pulled the plastic bag out of his shirt and emptied his hands into it. He went back to the bushes, filled the bag until it was stuffed, then placed it back inside his shirt again.

When Anthony picked up his walking stick, he recalled his decision last night to find a sturdier stick. So he climbed the hillside until he came onto a clump of small bushes. He found a suitable sapling, and whittled a ring around the bottom of it. The wood was hard, but he whittled until the ring was deep enough that he could break the sapling off. He held the stick upright to judge where he should cut off the top, and again he whittled it down to where he could break it off. Those two broken ends would have to be smoothed off, but he could do that during his rest periods.

Now he faced a major decision. Should he continue to search for a way home, and possibly forget his way back to a ready supply of food and his tree home? Or, should he stay in the general area, never getting too far from this creek, the one that could always guide him back?

After he considered all the angles, he decided to stay in this general area while the folks back home continued to search for him. He knew they had not given up looking. He had found that out last night. And maybe the helicopter would come again. If it did, he would try to be where they could see him. He would wave his white handkerchief at them, maybe put it on the end of his walking stick and wave it up high.

With his mind made up, he ate one more small paw-paw and returned to the creek. He continued up the trail, just as he had previously intended to do. He could go quite a distance and still keep within sight of the creek. That way he could always find his way back to food and his tree house. He felt it might be a long time before he found another shelter like the hollow sycamore.

He had another idea. If he could find a high point on one of the ridges that butted down to the creek, he could climb up where he could be seen readily and spend the days there. Then, at the end of the day he could come back, find his way back to the paw-paw tree, then to his shelter.

He set off up the trail by the creek and had travelled hardly a quarter mile when he saw a ridge, up to his left and jutting out from the main portion of the mountain, that looked to be almost bare of trees. It might be a likely place where he could be readily seen by the helicopter. So up he went.

He was surprised at the absence of trees on the ridge, since farther up the mountain, and on the steep sides of the ridge, there was a heavy growth of timber. As he checked the area out, he could see a rather large branch at the foot of the far slope. Maybe, he thought, just maybe there could be another old house seat down there by the spring. Not likely another old orchard, but you would never know unless you checked. He could come right back up the way he had gone down, and he wouldn't lose his bearings. He didn't want to be lost again. One time was quite enough.

The slope proved to be very steep. There was a lot of downed timber, which he slowly worked his way through. At the bottom, he found a very active source of water, but no old house seat.

He decided to get a drink while he was there. When he got down to the water he saw bees -- dozens of them -- honey bees. This was the watering hole for a hive of wild honey bees. They would have a hive nearby, in a hollow tree deep in the mountains He was familiar with such a situation, for he and his Dad had coursed wild honey bees in forest lands a few times before. It had been something fun that they could do together. It was almost like a sport, trying to outfox those little honey makers at their own game of hide-go-seek.

The bees, loaded with water until their flight was slowed, would come up, circle, then set off in a straight line for their tree hive.

The more Anthony watched, the greater his excitement grew. He could readily see their course to the top of the next ridge where they were passing just to the left of a towering red spruce tree.

The excitement of the game took hold of him. He would go to that red spruce and see if he could get a further line on the little flyers' course. So down he went, sliding on the slope.

The slope grew steeper as he went. His walking stick was almost useless so he found himself clinging to trees and bits of scrub undergrowth until he reached the valley.

Going up to the top of the next ridge was even more difficult. He climbed over a shale break that slid out from under his feet. There was less low growth in the rocky shale that he could pull himself along with.

When he reached the red spruce, he had no trouble sighting the bees' path as they crossed the top of the ridge. They were dropping slightly, but not enough to indicate that their hive would be on the near slope. It would be, from all indications, on the face of the next rise. He had come this far, why not check just one more ridge? Then he could turn around and retrace the way he had come. That way he would not get lost.

This time, he was faced with an even steeper slope, but he negotiated it, albeit with much slipping and sliding. When he got to the bottom, he found himself in a very deep ravine.

When he started up the other side he found it to be even steeper still. But he could clearly see the tree on the course he was following. Using his walking stick and pulling on some sprouts, he began clawing his way up the mountain side.

About half way up to the tree, he grasped a rotting log to help him pull up.

The top of the log broke off, revealing a whole passel of tiny blacksnakes. The mother snake had laid her eggs in the rotten wood inside the log and the eggs were now hatching.

Anthony watched the wiggling little creatures for a minute or so, then placed the top of the log back over them. That cover would protect them from predators until they could scatter, one by one, out into the forest about them.

Finally he reached the guide tree, a red oak, very tall and straight but without a sign of a hole in it. It certainly was not the bee tree he was looking for. So he climbed on higher.

He had climbed about twenty feet further up, and there it was, right on the line he had selected. Anthony was jubilant. He had walked almost directly to the tree hive. The hive tree was a medium size white walnut, sometimes referred to as butternut, with a hole in it about ten feet up. And there were the bees -- dozens of them, all about the entrance and a constant flight of them coming and going. There were a number of dead limbs on the tree. It was dying. There would be a large hollow inside the tree which would account for the large number of bees. It had to be a strong hive.

Anthony stood for a moment, admiring his find. He had done it all by himself. What a story he would have to tell his Dad when he got home! All that honey, right there inside this tree. If he had a way of getting to that bundle of sweetness, what a feast he would have!

Anthony had studied about bees. He knew that here was a busy lot of chemists

- workers who knew just how to combine the water some of the bees brought with the nectar gathered by others to make that heavenly tasting syrup known as honey. Other bees were busy making perfectly shaped wax cells from the pollen gathered on the legs of still other bees. Those cells formed the containers in which the honey was stored.

Yet, gloating over his success would get him nowhere, and wishing would get him no honey. Right now, he needed to point himself back the way he had come, if he could remember the way.

He had been so engrossed in the course he was following that he had paid no attention to the surroundings about him as he travelled. He knew that was a bad thing to do. Still, he could see that red spruce he had sighted on earlier, standing out clear on the first ridge he had come over. So, at least he wasn't lost -- just yet.

Anthony began his trek back up the course. When he got down into the ravine, he looked up at the steep ridge he had slid down just a while before. He knew it would be a difficult climb, so he began looking for a way around it. Negotiating the steep hillsides had wearied him.

If he followed the ravine down to the butt of the ridge, he could go around it. There he could find the heavy branch that he had first come down to check. If he followed it down, he would soon find his way back to the creek. So down he went, stumbling in the rough terrain surrounding the little branch as it wended its way down the ravine. At times, when both sides of the valley were very steep, he had to wade in the branch.

He soon came to a place where the steep ridge to his right leveled off, so he decided to short cut across that level and pick up the stream again.

He had travelled only a short distance until he came to a small branch. It wasn't a tenth the size of the stream he had expected to find. What had happened to that big flow of water? Was he lost again?

That feeling of despair that had hit him the first time he admitted to himself that he was lost came back like a flash. But it haunted him only briefly.

He turned up this smaller stream and followed it to where the crest of the ridge broke over an extended rock outcrop. There, at the base of the outcrop he found a small spring.

From his position on the ridge, Anthony could see that, over a period of many years, that small branch had simply divided the main ridge into two smaller ones.

He went on around the second ridge, and there was the big stream he was looking for, just as large as it had been up at the spring where he had found the bees.

He followed the big branch only a short distance until it crossed the game trail and emptied into a creek. This had to be his creek. He turned to the right and headed back toward his tree house.

He had travelled hardly a quarter mile when he heard a soft cry, much like that of a baby in distress. But there could be no baby out here in the wilderness. It had to be some animal. Or maybe a strange bird that he had never heard call before.

He searched along the trail, but found nothing. Then he heard the cry again, now behind him. He had missed something.

He turned back, and looked on both sides of the trail and up in the trees, where maybe a baby bird was stranded.

He was about to give up when he saw the panther kitten. It lay on a narrow strip of land between the trail and the creek. It was watching him intently

Why was the little animal lying on it's side? Was it hurt? There had to be some reason why it did not run away, when it could certainly see him so very near. It followed his every move.

When Anthony stepped down from the trail, the little creature tried to leap away but fell on its side. That was when Anthony saw the trap clinging to the kitten's left rear foot.

"You little guy," Anthony said. "You should not be out here alone in this wilderness. I'll help you out of that trap. Then you can go back to your mommy, wherever she is. She must be missing you."

He had once seen his father help a cat out of a trap by finding a dead limb and compressing the trap spring. Now Anthony searched until he found a stick. But when he approached the kitten it tried to leap away again.

The little panther had never been so near a man creature before, one that stood erect on two legs. This one didn't look dangerous, but he remembered the two men he had seen on the mountain shortly after his mother had been killed.

And he had heard their sticks go off with a loud bang and had seen squirrels fall dead after each bang.

Now here was this man creature, with a stick in his hands, Besides, all animals larger than himself were to be feared, and this one was much bigger. So he was frightened and ready to defend himself the best he could. His ears were flattened on the top of his head and his lips curled to show his white kitten teeth.

Anthony didn't want the little fellow to damage his foot further, so he paused for a few minutes.

"Just take it easy, little fellow," Anthony said. "I'll see if I can get you out of that contraption."

Anthony continued talking softly to the panther kitten. It seemed to relax. Its ears came back up and its eyes opened wide. The lips ceased to curl.

Moving very slowly, Anthony eased the stick onto the trap spring, then bore down gently. The jaws of the trap parted, and the kitten's foot fell free.

The panther kitten leaped away, then turned. He watched the man creature throw the stick aside, saw him take out his knife and cut the meat bait down.

The kitten was hungry. He wanted that meat. But now, was that man creature going to eat the meat? That was what any other animal of his world would do. That was what he expected Anthony to do. If the man creature had been any other animal, he might have been willing to fight for the food. He was mystified by what was happening right there in front of him.

The man creature had made no move to hurt him. Rather, he had set him free of that thing that had held him captive and had caused much pain to his foot. Now the man had gotten the food that the kitten had wanted so badly but could not reach. And now the man creature was offering it to him.

A step at a time, the little kitten came forward. He watched the man set the meat down and step back. The man creature was still making those sounds, sounds that were soothing rather than frightening. Saber grabbed the meat and tore at it frantically.

Anthony waited patiently until the kitten had downed the entire chunk of meat. As small as the little panther's stomach had to be, that bait had certainly filled it.

CHAPTER 10

It now seemed to Anthony that it was time for he and the panther kitten to each go their own way. Still, he had enjoyed the presence of the little animal. Maybe he didn't feel quite so alone for those few minutes that he had been around the kitten. However, he climbed back into the trail and started walking away.

The kitten had feelings similar to those of Anthony. For brief minutes he had experienced a new kind of friendship. It was a strange feeling for him. The man creature had shown no desire to harm him, but instead had helped him. The man creature had gotten him out of the thing that was holding him captive, causing great pain to his foot. And he had not only gotten the food for him, but he had calmed him with those soothing sounds. When he saw the man thing going away, he climbed up into the trail, favoring his damaged foot, and hastened to catch him.

When Anthony looked back, he saw the panther kitten close to his heels. Almost immediately he had a feeling of closeness to that little creature. He needed a companion, the panther kitten needed the same. They were suddenly friends by association and need.

"You're a panther," Anthony said. "I once read a story about a panther named Saber. So I'm naming you Saber."

Although pleased at finding a new found friend, it seemed to Anthony that right now he had too many decisions to make. He must decide which ridge to climb up, to find a place where he could be seen, in case the helicopter came again. Also, he wanted to see the trapper when he came to check his trapline. If the man looked trustworthy, Anthony might ask him how to get out of this vast wilderness that was now holding him a veritable prisoner, or maybe even get the trapper to take him out.

But that would bring on a big decision.

The trapper was looking for skins to put on stretching frames in his fur shed. He would want Saber's hide. And Anthony would have no way of stopping him. So what would he do then? He would have to weigh his escape from the forest against the life of his new found friend. It would be a momentous decision. For already, as the little creature tagged along behind him, he was becoming more attached to the panther kitten.

Then too, Saber trusted him or he would not be following him. How could you betray that kind of trust?

Anthony turned to the right and began climbing the ridge above the trapping scene. This was his first decision. He would take the others on when it came time to do so. Right now he was looking for a way home, a way out of this wild land that had so completely claimed him.

As Anthony climbed the steep slope, the little panther keep in step with him, sometimes leading a bit. On top they found a rocky patch devoid of trees. This would be perfect if the helicopter returned. Also, Anthony could see the trail below, in case the trapper came by checking his traps.

Since both Anthony and the panther kitten were well fed for the day, they were content to rest. Both were now well into their fourth day of constant travel, and it was beginning to tell on them. Anthony found a pillow of leaves the wind had built up against a fallen tree and sat down. Saber came up to him, curled up in the leaves beside him, and went to sleep.

The afternoon came and went, but no trapper was to be seen on the trail below. Nor was there a helicopter within hearing. Had he expected a helicopter? Well maybe not, but he had hoped for one.

Saber became restless before Anthony was ready to head home, so he began checking the area. He heard squeaking sounds beside a fallen tree log. When he dug back the leaves and dirt, he uncovered a nest of baby white breasted mountain mice. They were tiny little hairless red creatures, hadn't opened their eyes yet, crawling around over each other.

Saber rolled one of the little mice out of the nest and ate it. He liked the taste, so he rolled the other six out, one at a time, and ate them all.

When the sun began to kiss the mountain tops to the west, Anthony decided it was time to go home. The two hurried down the ridge to the trail and turned right. They stopped by the paw-paw patch, where Anthony ate a couple fruits. He offered one to Saber, who wanted nothing to do with the yellow fruit.

THE LOST BOY

At the tree house Saber followed at once when Anthony crawled inside. The little panther kitten curled up in the leaves along the back wall and was soon asleep.

Anthony listened to the night come in. There was the final scolding of a fox squirrel high up in one of the trees, the brief song fest of the wood thrushes, then that sacred hour of twilight, complete silence. That was followed by the katydids and other night insects that seemed to create a chorus just for Anthony and the kitten.

A frog thumped from the creek, and then they heard the feared yapping of coyotes. Anthony got his walking stick handy in case they were molested, but no attack came. The coyotes went away, but the katydids continued their rasping tunes.

It was not the coyotes that disturbed Anthony the most, it was the trapper. He wanted to go home, yet how had he become so attached to this little wild animal? But he had. And he had that fact to deal with.

Another thing that had been bothering Anthony was what his parents were going through. He knew they were frantic, that they were searching the wilderness both day and night. But had they done the one thing he felt sure would result in his coming home? Had they gone to Agnes Long and had her pray for his return?

Because of her great faith, many residents of Cave Creek Valley went to Agnes with their problems. And when Agnes deemed their situation sufficient to ask God's help, they always got it.

Certainly, his parents had gone to Agnes. Or had they? He was still here, still lost in the wilds of that fabled land: The Monongahela.

At last, tired and weary, he went to sleep, dreaming of a way home.

CHAPTER 11

Sometime during the night Anthony came out of his tree house into the trail. A full moon flooded the forest, lighting it to nearly the brilliance of day, and there were no frightening sounds to disturb him.

Anthony began walking up the trail. He wasn't sure what he was looking for, but he was looking, along the trail, up the hollows that spread out between neighboring ridges. Then he saw a faint light nestled back between two ridges, possibly a hundred yards away.

He turned from the trail and hesitated for long moments before he began walking toward the light. When he got close he could see a weathered log cabin. Closer still, and he could see that the light was coming from a small stained window glass.

He stood there for a few minutes wondering what to do. The building was small, it had a thatched roof, it could well be a trapper's cabin. Maybe it was the cabin used by the trapper who had set out the line where Saber had been caught. If it was, he might be creating another problem by going farther. He faltered for several minutes, letting a series of "Might be's" race through his mind.

Anthony had come this far. He had to know If it was someone who just lived this far back in the wilderness, or if it was the trapper he feared. Possibly, it would be someone who could show him the way home. So, he moved closer to the door, cautiously, a step at a time.

He knocked, a timid little knock. The door opened almost at once and he found himself facing a small stooped man with soft blue eyes and a heavily grayed beard.

"Do come in," the man said in a soft charming voice that put Anthony at ease immediately.

"You poor dear," he added. "You must certainly be lost, or you would not be out here wandering around in the night."

"I am lost," Anthony said as he entered the cabin. "I have been lost for several days now. I have searched all over but I can't find my way home. When I saw the light in your window I thought that you might be able to tell me how to get home."

"That's what I am here for," the old man said as he seated himself on the side of a bed and motioned Anthony to come sit beside him.

"Are you the trapper that set out the traps down on the creek?" Anthony asked.

"Goodness no," the man said. "I wouldn't do anything like that." He said with emphasis. "I would never do anything to hurt the wild animals. I live with them. They are my friends."

"But," Anthony paused, "do you live back here all the time?"

"The great wild reaches of the Monongahela are my land, my home," the old man said. " Yes, I live back here all the time, if you want to call it that. This is my home."

"But," Anthony paused again. "Why do you live so far away from everyone?"

"I'm not far away," the old man said. "I'm here where I have been for many years, where I belong, where I have to stay. And you, where is your home?"

Anthony started to explain in detail where he lived but the old man stopped him.

"I'm Tabby Tambourine," the old man said. "I know all the area around where you live. We'll get you home. It will take a couple days so we best get some sleep. We will want to get an early start tomorrow."

"You said where you have to stay," Anthony questioned. "Why do you have to stay away up here, wherever we are?"

"It's a long story," Tabby said. "But since you asked maybe I should tell you. It all happened a long time ago, probably before your Dad was born, maybe even many years before that. It has been so long that I have lost track of time.

"Back then I lived in a community something like the one you live in. I was a respected citizen. Everything seemed so right. Then a friend of mine, who was an alcoholic, killed a child in a fit of anger while he was drunk.

"Somehow that friend was able to convince everyone that I was the guilty party. So the community decided to hang me. They took me out to the woods and strung me up to a tree. But since I was not the guilty one, the rope broke and set me free so that I could escape into the wilds of the Monongahela.

"So, for all of these years, maybe even a hundred, I don't know, I have devoted myself to finding lost children in the forest and getting them home. So you will just be another one that I have helped. But there is something that I must ask you to do for me."

"I'll do anything you ask if you will just get me home," Anthony said.

"You must not tell anyone who helped you home or where I live," Tabby said.

"I'll certainly do what you are asking me to do," Anthony said.

Now he saw the old man nestle down in a heap of leaves on his bed.

"You can sleep in that box of leaves over in the corner," Tabby said. "That is where my dog Ranger slept before he left me.

"Tomorrow, as we travel, I will tell you all about Ranger and the many things he did for me, and with me, as I lived here alone, with no one to help me when things went wrong.

"I'll show you where I buried Ranger after he died from a snake bite and I want you to see the great tree that grew at the head of his grave."

When Tabby quit talking, he appeared to doze off.

Anthony looked at the box of leaves. It was very small. Yet he wanted to do what the old man told him to do. He wanted Tabby Tambourine to help him get out of this wilderness, to get back home where he belonged. So he curled himself up in the box of leaves and went to sleep.

CHAPTER 12

Day five came with a bang. Anthony heard what sounded like a small rifle, possibly a .22 caliber. He was awake immediately. He sat up and looked around. He wasn't in a box of leaves. Where was Tabby Tambourine? Then he saw the opening in his tree house. He felt in the leaves and found Saber.

There had been no Tabby Tambourine. That had all been a dream. And now, something was happening out there on the trail, close to his tree house.

Saber had heard the shot. It brought back bad memories of that fateful day when he had lost his mother to such a noise. He crowded against the back wall of the tree home and snuggled down in the leaves.

Anthony suspected that it was the trapper they had heard. He knew the panther kitten was frightened, and he didn't want him to try to run away.

He stretched himself in front of Saber and maneuvered his head so he could see the trail in front of the opening in the hollow sycamore. If someone passed by, he wanted to get a good look at him.

It was several minutes before Anthony heard steps clumping along the trail. Then he watched a pair of legs as they passed by. When he thought it was safe, he scooted around so he could see the man.

He was a big man wearing slouchy clothes with his pants tucked into what appeared to be waterproof boots. And his body kind of dipped as he walked. In his left hand he was carrying a small rifle. In the other hand was a dead raccoon. Apparently that coon was what he had shot.

About thirty or forty feet down the trail was a big rock. The man lay the coon on the rock and dropped down the bank toward the creek. He wasn't gone long. When he came back, he was carrying a mink.

The trapper sat down on the rock and took a knife out of his pocket and began skinning his catch.

First, he skinned the mink and threw the carcass down over the bank. The coon soon followed, and he discarded the carcass the same way. He placed the pelts in a sack over his shoulder, picked up his rifle, and clumped away.

In those brief moments Anthony had looked the man over carefully. His clothes were dirty and ragged. His hair was long. It came out from under a fur cap and hung over the collar of his coat. But his face was what turned Anthony off. There was such a heavy beard that all he could see were two eyes and a nose. A stained mustache completely covered his mouth.

Anthony decided that he would not want to be alone with that man anywhere, especially deep in the wilderness. So the main problem that had plagued him until well into the night had solved itself.

It was several minutes before Anthony came out of the tree house. He wanted to be sure that the trapper was well away. He couldn't get the image of that man out of his mind. And he was sure of one thing -- he wanted nothing to do with the man he had seen, even if it had meant a way home.

The panther kitten was still crowded as far back in the tree home as he could get. Anthony decided to leave him there while he retrieved the coon carcass.

Down over the bank, just opposite the big rock, Anthony found what was to feed Saber for the day. He took out his knife and opened it. He split the belly of the coon carcass and took out the entrails. That way the meat would keep fresh longer.

The things that Anthony remembered from walking and hunting with his Dad continued to help him while he learned to survive in the wilderness.

He then found a small green sprout, cut out a stick about eight inches long and sharpened both ends. He picked up the coon by the heels and drove one sharpened end of his stick between the big leader back of the heel and the leg bone. He did likewise with the other end of the stick and the other leg. He now had a handle to carry the carcass without messing up his hands.

Down at the creek, Anthony washed his knife and put it away. Then he washed his hands and dried them on his pants leg.

He returned to the trail, picking up the coon carcass with his improvised handle. With it, he was able to entice Saber out of the tree house.

Day five's travel for the two vagabonds had now begun. The first stop was the paw-paw patch. All the way Saber had kept his eye on the fresh meat that his buddy carried. And when Anthony found a clean spot to lay it down, the kitten sailed into his breakfast with a vigor.

While Saber stuffed himself, Anthony ate some fresh paw-paws. He then emptied the two old fruits from his plastic bag, refilled it with fresh ones, and put it back inside his shirt.

With breakfast over, Anthony wanted to get well away from the trapline. Somehow that thing had soured his respect for the greatness of the wilderness, and he wanted it behind him. Far behind him. They would have to find another shelter. It would be a long time before they would find another place like the hollow sycamore, but they would try.

Somewhere, there would be a shallow cave, or a secluded recess in the vast rock formations that were ever present in the mountains. And as for security, Anthony was already practicing the art of wielding his much heavier walking stick. He felt he could already feel new strength in his arms, just from the limited practice he had done.

Anthony paused beside the paw-paw patch and smiled to himself. What a change the little panther kitten had made in his thinking. During those first lost days his thinking had always been about "Me." Now his plans were always about "We." He was no longer alone in the wilderness, and somehow it seemed so very good to him.

They chose to go on up the draw above the paw-paw patch. They climbed, working their way through a valley of tumbled boulders until they reached a steep mountain abutment where they found a bubbly little spring that came out from beneath a massive sandstone formation.

Anthony had long ago learned to drop down on his hands and knees to drink. So, while he sipped from the spring, little Saber lapped from the branch that splashed down it's steep rocky way.

The mountain abruptly ahead of them was so steep that they turned to their left and angled around the slope until they reached the top of the adjoining ridge.

There Anthony found, spread out across the flat top of the ridge, an open place where a rock ledge had limited the trees. This, he determined, would be a place where the helicopter would have no trouble seeing them if it came back. He was fearful that it would never come back. Yet he could still hope, and hope he did.

The sun had driven away the chill of the night, warming the rocks and making them pleasant to rest on. A gentle breeze caressed the ridge top and brought a few colorful leaves floating down. It was a perfect fall day. So the two vagabonds, with their middles stuffed, were content to just relax a bit before continuing the day's hunt.

They listened to squirrels scolding from the trees as they searched for nuts to hide away for winter. A hungry little broad winged hawk screeched overhead as it searched the forest floor for something to swoop down upon. Small birds flitted into heavy bushes in an effort to hide from the hawk. Squirrels flattened themselves on top of limbs and became silent and motionless.

Everything seemed normal to the two, resting on the rocks, until a deer came racing down the back of the ridge and passed them by. A few noisy jays set up a chatter somewhere up the back of the ridge. They were apparently scolding something. Then the squirrels became suddenly quiet again.

All of these signs caught the attention of both the boy and the panther kitten. Something was amiss.

Anthony stood up and got a firm grip on his walking stick. He was glad now that he had a more sturdy stick. He practiced whipping it around a couple times and liked the feel of it.

Saber crowded in against his companion's leg. No doubt he was catching something in the air currents that Anthony could not read.

Two coyotes came slinking quietly down before the rock ledge. Already they had their eyes on the pair. A step at a time, the coyotes came forward.

Anthony looked around to see if there might be a better place to fight from. Then he got a second shock. Behind him were three more coyotes, close together, slinking toward the rock where Anthony and the kitten had sought safety. Their mouths hung open. Saliva dripped from their jaws, their stained teeth bared. There was no question what their intentions were.

Anthony screamed. The panther baby let out a tiny cry. Anthony screamed again. But the screaming did nothing to stop, or even to slow the coyotes.

Suddenly, Anthony stopped screaming. A memory of a story he had heard many times about the time Old Crooked Toe saved the Long children from the wild dog pack flashed through his mind.

THE LOST BOY

He threw back his head and in a loud voice cried, "Please, God help us."

Before he could even open his eyes, he heard a bellow so loud and so close that it seemed almost to shake the rock the two of them were standing on.

PART III
CHAPTER 13

Shortly before his mate was shot down, Old Crooked Toe had experienced one of those dry spells when nothing seemed to click. He had gone three days without a kill, not even a squirrel, when the woods were full of them. It wasn't that there was no big game. The deer were plentiful. There had been a bumper crop of young fawns last spring. It was simply that he had not been at the right place at the right time.

So it was that for three days there had been no food to drop over the ledge above the den that housed his mate and his baby.

Then he struck. It was a big buck, but it came with some effort. He had travelled almost a mile down out of the great peaks to a point where two main game trails crossed. Just above the junction of the two trails was a bluff at the base of one of the northern ridges. It was so situated, that from its top the old panther could leap off onto either of the trails where they crossed. And it was on that bluff that Old Crooked Toe had waited for more than five hours before what he wanted came along.

He had seen fawns, a small doe, a red fox and many squirrels, even a small bear. Still the old panther waited. He wanted meat, lots of meat. And then it came.

It was a buck deer, a big buck deer. It sported a massive set of antlers. Its back was broad and flat. The hips, the rear quarters, where the meat was, were well rounded and massive.

Old Crooked Toe tensed when he saw the buck coming, but not even a whisker moved. Big old bucks were cautious, suspicious creatures, easily spooked. And he had waited five hours for this moment, this very special animal.

When the buck was at the right place, Old Crooked Toe sprang, but even as he leaped the deer heard him and threw up his head.

The panther had intended to land on the neck, but instead he was met by a maze of antler tines that threw him off his mark. He was knocked to the ground, but his weight had brought the buck to his knees.

The deer, however, was big and strong. He was up and on his feet before the panther could get to his throat.

The only thing Old Crooked Toe had time to grab was a front leg. As the buck leaped, the weight of the panther on his leg threw him on his side. That was all that Old Crooked Toe needed. He was at the buck's throat in a flash. When the buck got to his feet again, blood was squirting from both sides of his neck. He ran a short way up the trail, with the panther following only a step behind. With the rapid loss of blood, the buck made it little more than a hundred yards before he dropped.

Old Crooked Toe dragged the still kicking carcass off the side of the trail and behind a thicket where he could feast in seclusion. He was not just hungry, he was famished. He intended to stuff himself before he cut out one of those massive hams to take to his charges. He opened the middle so he could get at the liver and heart. Then he lay down beside the kill and proceeded to gorge himself.

Soon it was time to get meat for his waiting mate and young. He tore out a rear quarter and skinned it. He bit off the leg bone and discarded the bone. That would lighten the load he was going to have to carry almost a mile.

He drug the remainder of the kill a little deeper into the woods and buried it with brush and leaves. Maybe he would return to the kill, maybe not. The act of burying the leftovers he did mostly by habit. It was a trait of his kind, to hide the remains for another day.

With a heavy load of meat dangling from his mouth, Old Crooked Toe began the long journey to the lair where his family was housed. He needed to hurry, yet he knew he would have to rest along the way.

And rest he did. Four times before he reached the boulder strewn peak that sported the lair of his charges, he dropped down in the trail and rested for several minutes. Each time he licked drippings from his forelegs and paws.

Old Crooked Toe had been cautious all summer long when approaching the secret lair where his mate was rearing his young. So, today, he used the path winding through a small field of boulders. It was well hidden by a heavy patch of low brush, so thick that the tops of the bushes formed a cover over the trail.

When he reached the ledge above the lair entrance, he purred softly. That usually brought two hungry heads out on the ledge below him, but not today.

He dropped the chunk of fresh kill down before the den opening. Nothing happened. He purred again. Still no response. This was not normal. A tingling of fear crept into his ancient brain.

He went around the hillside, dropping down to the path the mother panther used in coming and going from the Den. There was no fresh scent. He came back around to the crevice in the cliff face. It was empty and there was no evidence of recent life.

He turned onto the path his mate and young had used all summer long on their normal daily hunts. It brought him around through the next draw. He found no scent to indicate that the path had been used recently and it was beginning to concern him.

He paused momentarily and scanned the steep slopes about him. Then he moved onto the bold hump above the valley. There he found the decaying remains of his mate.

The old panther had spent close to three decades in the wilds of the Monongahela. He was well schooled in the happenings of his world. He immediately chalked his loss up to human hunters, the kind that had stalked him so many times over his long life, in the deep dark isles of the land he knew as home.

For brief moments the old panther was overcome by fierce anger. The she-panther was the only mate he had known in all of his years. And the little panther kitten was the only one he had ever fathered.

He lifted his great head and screamed. It was a terrible cry, filled with anger and laced with sorrow. It echoed across the valley, shattering the stillness of the forest in every direction. It sent squirrels scampering for cover, and scattered birds throughout the valley.

He paused briefly, listening to his cry fade in the distance. Then he went looking for the little kitten that he felt should be somewhere near.

He found no remains of the young panther. Surely it had escaped the hunters and would be hiding, possibly in a dense thicket on the slope above where his mother had been killed.

He made a wide semi-circle about the ridge above where the she-panther had been killed, but found nothing. When he came down to the ravine on the far side of the bold hump, he found a leaf with the faint trace of the little kitten on it. Then another. But the trail had grown faint with time, and the wind and falling leaves made it impossible to follow.

At least he had a direction. It pointed a course toward the top of the mountain, and that was where he hastened.

On a normal day, the old panther would be curled on a rock or maybe on some high point, sleeping off a full stomach and soaking up the brilliant sunlight that bathed the forest this morning. But not today. He did not see the squirrel that ran away before him. He did not hear the noisy jays scolding from the trees above. He was on a mission. He was of one mind set -- To find his baby before it fell prey to one of the hungry predators that infested the wilderness at every turn.

CHAPTER 14

As the old panther began his mission he was certain of only one thing. His little offspring was out there somewhere, in a wild and dangerous world, alone, probably frightened and most certainly hungry. He felt also that this would probably be the longest stalk of his life. But he knew he would do it.

He reached the top of the mountain and turned down the slope toward the valley. He slowed his pace, scanning the forest about him as he found his way down the hill.

When he started up the next slope, he found the hunter's stand. There was still the faint odor where they had been seated on a log, and he found two cigarette butts and three spent shell casings.

The fury that had overcome the old panther when he saw the remains of his dead mate welled up in him again. If he could have gotten at those two hunters at that moment, he would have charged them so fast that they would have had no opportunity to use their rifles. But they were not there. Nothing was there for him to vent his anger on. He growled viciously and turned away.

He resumed his climb up the steep slope and continued down the other side. He was making a thorough search of both sides of the mountain, all the way down to the valley on the far side and back again.

Twice he jumped deer, but gave them no heed. Once he surprised a wood-chuck away from his den, but let him get away. He had no interest in food today. He was no longer searching for a kill. His mind was intent only on the task at hand: finding his lost kitten somewhere out there, in a land filled with hungry predators. Finding him before one of those scavengers could make a meal of him.

He was on the far side of the mountain when the buzz of a rattler stopped him. He teased the snake and jumped back as it struck. When its body landed stretched out in the trail, he scooped it up with a forepaw and sent it flying out through the brush. At last he had found something to vent his anger on.

As he came up the back side of the mountain he had a frightening thought. Maybe the hunters had captured the kitten after killing his mother and had carried him away.

He hurried back to the spot where the hunters had rested and shot from. What he wanted to know was where the men had gone after they left. He had no trouble following the trail the two hunters had made when they climbed back up the hill. There were disturbed leaves where they had dragged their feet, and also a faint odor of man. It was so strong that he had no trouble reading it.

He followed their trail all the way to the top of the mountain and then about half way down the back side. That convinced him that they had not gone to the den. If there had been serious indication that the hunters had carried off his offspring, the old panther would have followed their trail to wherever they lived. That did not seem to be the case, so he went back to the top of the mountain to continue his search.

On his next swing down the mountain he crossed the broad valley, searching the hills on the other side. He lapped a bit of water as he crossed back over the brook that wended its way down the valley, then climbed back up the mountain to continue making his circles again.

It was on this swing up that he found where the little panther had killed the woodchuck. The bones, hide and head of the chuck were still there. Here was the strongest scent of the kitten that he had found so far. Finally he had a place to start from.

Finding the scene of Saber's kill gave the old panther new hope. His little offspring was definitely learning to hunt. It would help the kitten survive until he could catch up with him.

The trail was weak, but with some patience he was able to get a direction. He circled out ahead and kept criss-crossing until he found a trace of scent on a leaf. This led him eventually to the great fallen tree where the little panther had spent the night.

He found the pillow of leaves where the kitten had slept. The scent was strong here, stronger than any he had found, and it was encouraging. His baby had certainly survived his first days alone in the wilderness.

It was now near nightfall, and Old Crooked Toe had spent the full day hunting, then carrying the heavy meat for close to a mile. Then, without rest, he had searched the wilderness for a full day. His weary old muscles were near exhaustion.

Maybe the kitten had taken up residence here and would return again for the night. So he decided to take a rest and wait the night out. He curled up on the pile of leaves that his baby had slept on and was soon asleep.

There soon followed the usual sounds of evening, then the twilight hour, and finally, the rasping of the katydids. But none of that concerned Old Crooked Toe. Later, when two wildcats somewhere out on the mountain had a disagreement over a kill, it never disturbed his slumber.

CHAPTER 15

The next morning, the old panther, fully rested and ready to go, was out of bed before daybreak. He began searching immediately, even before the rising sun had caressed the mountain tops.

He found enough faint scent to point him down the mountain. He determined immediately that the kitten had no intention of finding his way back to the lair.

Since he was close to his kill of a few days ago, he found his way back to where he had covered the remains of the big buck. But when he broke through the brush, he saw that the cover had been torn back and two coyotes were nibbling on his kill. He was infuriated.

He hated coyotes, and the sight of them chewing on his own dinner added new sparks to the fire. He lunged out with a frantic growl that could be heard a half mile away. The coyotes almost ran over each other in their haste to get away. Old Crooked Toe followed them only a short distance. When he was sure they were gone, he came back, lay down beside the remains of the buck and feasted.

He normally would have rested somewhere near his kill, but not today. He was back on the search, invigorated by a full maw.

As he stepped back onto the hard beaten trail, he came face to face with a bear.

It was a big bear with a nasty disposition, eager for a fight. And the old panther was still smarting over the loss of his mate. He was in no mood to give quarter.

As the bear charged, Old Crooked Toe leaped aside, spun around and raked the bear with his needle sharp claws. He cut through hair and skin all the way down from the bear's shoulder to his elbow.

The strike did nothing to stop the bear: in fact, it only enraged him. The bear came back with another charge, and once again the panther dodged aside, raking the ribs and belly of his assailant.

This time however, the bear's response was quicker. He caught the panther with a blow from his heavy right arm, sending him rolling out into the brush.

Now it was Old Crooked Toe's turn to be completely enraged. He drove at the bear so fast that the big brute had no time to respond, catching the bear with a blow just back of the ear that sent him down.

In a flash the panther was at his assailant's throat, tearing at skin and flesh. The bear, now on his back, tried to fight back with his feet, but the old panther had fought many bears in his time. He was familiar with what those rear feet could do. He slipped aside, baring down and chewing on the bear's throat.

Like all wild animals, the bear, knew he had to protect his throat at all costs. He doubled up his body and gave a great heave, simultaneously breaking the panther's grip while the bear rolled up onto his feet.

The bear decided that retreat was the better part of valor. He had had enough for one day. The old panther watched as the bear loped away at top speed, leaving drops of blood on the hard packed earth.

Probably, in one of the far reaches of the Monongahela, that bear was also a king. That was why he had been so eager for a fight. But he was on his way back to his own domain now.

Old Crooked Toe did not pursue the bear. He had won the battle. On top of that, he had found a willing assailant to vent his anger on; anger that had built up inside him since he had first found the remains of his dead mate. That anger had needed a way out, and the bear had furnished it.

When Old Crooked Toe was assured that the bear was headed out of his territory, he turned again to the pressing mission at hand, finding the lost kitten. The encounter with the coyotes and the bear had placed a greater emphasis on the need to find his young helpless offspring before such critters as these happened onto him.

He crossed the valley, lapping up a bit of water from the brook, then climbed rapidly up the mountain to the spot where he had last found evidence of the panther kitten.

At least he had a general direction to proceed in. That direction indicated that the kitten was still intent on putting more distance between himself and the horrific death of his mother that he had so recently witnessed.

Banking on that conclusion, Old Crooked Toe struck a course that carried him to the peak of the mountain, then down a steep butt on the other side. He was about half way down the slope when he heard a clap of thunder in the distance.

He had been concentrating on his search so intently that he had been unaware of the dark clouds rolling in. The old panther dodged the rain any time he could, and he now turned his attention to finding one of his many secret retreats. He was usually close to one of his shelters, regardless of where he was in the vast reaches of the great forest.

He swung around the hill and up a hollow. Soon he found a heavy clump of brush before a sandstone ledge. He dived into a cavity beneath the rock formation, just as he began to be peppered by big drops of rain.

In his haste, he almost landed on a wildcat that had sought shelter beneath the same rock. Of course, the wildcat sailed out into the rain and hurried away, in hopes of finding shelter somewhere else. He wasn't in a mood to spar with the rascal who had driven him into the rain, now coming down in great sheets.

The old panther settled himself onto a pillow of leaves that the wind had blown back into the opening. He listened to the thunder as the rain came in great waves, one after the other. While the storm pounded the mountainside, he rested, even dropping off to sleep despite the severe thunder and frightening streaks of lightning overhead.

When the storm was over, the old panther realized that the pounding rain had eliminated any faint trace of a trail. So, he determined to wait the night out in the dry.

Tomorrow he would get an early start. By making a series of wide circles he hoped to find fresh scent on the wet leaves. If he was right, that would be a trail he could follow readily. It would speed up his search, and he felt a need for speed.

He felt he was close to finding his lost offspring. He wasn't sure how many days the little kitten had been out there alone. But he was fully aware of the hazards the little one was facing.

Age was slowing the old panther in many ways. A full day of travel up and down the mountains had taken its toll on his old muscles. He listened to the coyotes yapping from a distant mountain top. He heard a pair of owls hooting at each other on the ridge, then he was lost to the other voices of the night.

CHAPTER 16

The new day came with the invigorating freshness that pervades the wilderness after a rain. The sun was bright, and the sweet smelling air filled the lungs of the old panther, rested and ready for a full day of activity. It would be a day consumed by only one purpose: finding the lost kitten.

Old Crooked Toe didn't know how far ahead of him the little panther was. But he felt he was gaining on his progeny. He began his first wide circle where he had left off the day before when the storm struck. He found nothing.

The second wide swing carried him all the way to the top of the opposite mountain. Again, nothing. Although he was unaware of it, he had missed the shelter the little panther had used during the storm by less than a hundred feet.

He went down the back side of that mountain, then crossed the next two mountains. His trek took him out of the territory that he claimed as his own. What Old Crooked Toe didn't realize was that he was invading the territory of a young panther he had once driven from Cave Creek Valley several years ago. This was the big cat the residents there had known as The Intruder. But that had been a long time ago, and neither of them had any memory of that previous incident.

THE LOST BOY

When Old Crooked Toe came upon The Intruder, the younger panther was the aggressor. This was his territory. He growled, spat, and threatened. Then he charged. But he was still the smaller of the two. And when Old Crooked Toe swatted him with a heavy forepaw, almost knocking him to the ground, he backed off.

Old Crooked Toe did not pursue. He was not interested in a fight just now. Another time, and he would have welcomed a good battle. So when the younger assailant withdrew, he turned back the way he had come, walking slowly. He didn't want to give the other panther the impression that he was running away from a good fight.

Old Crooked Toe knew that he had missed the trail. He had lost it close to where he had been when the storm struck. He had found no scent on any of his travels this day, and it was discouraging.

What had he missed? How much time had he lost?

So, still making small circles, he came back to the top of the mountain opposite where he had been when the storm rolled in. He stood there for several minutes, debating what to do next.

He had spent most of the day searching, to no avail. Night was coming in fast. Deepening shadows were slipping down the steep slopes of the mountains on all sides of him. So he went looking for shelter from the night. He needed a place to rest his weary body. And that was when he found the crevice under the rocks where Saber had sheltered during the storm.

Once again the old panther was exhausted from a long day. He slipped into the cavity and sacked in for the night. It was then he realized that the shelter he had taken was heavy with the odor of the one he was searching for.

In his younger years, the old panther would have come back out and hit the trail again. But he was not in his younger years. Time had caught up with him. A full day of climbing up and down the mountains had wearied Old Crooked Toe's aging carcass. So he nestled down in the bed his baby had used the night before. He would sleep the night out, and tomorrow he would be rested and ready to hit the trail early. Soon he was resting comfortably in a bed of leaves that was still heavy with the odor of his offspring.

It was not a restful night. Twice the old panther came out of his shelter when coyotes held a yapping fest on top of the mountain above him. On the second occasion he let out a scream that sent the culprits running away. But that was not all.

Apparently the coyotes had made a kill above his shelter, leaving some remains when they scooted away. That attracted the attention of a Barred Owl. Later, the Barred Owl had a verbal encounter with a Great Horned Owl challenging him for the remains of the coyote's kill. A loud squawking and flapping of wings ensued, but the encounter was soon over. The bigger and fiercer Great Horned Owl had prevailed.

CHAPTER 17

Daylight the following morning found Old Crooked Toe out of his shelter and on a trail that, at first, seemed easy to follow. But he soon found that the wind had so disturbed the leaves on the steep hillside that he was forced to make wide circles out ahead, just to stay on course.

Confused and impatient, he finally decided to keep a general course and drop on down to the hard packed game trail at the foot of the hill. Certainly he would find something there.

Much to his surprise, he found many odors in the trail. There was the special scent of the trapper. That was the strongest and most pervasive, certainly the scent of a full grown man, one who had not bathed recently. Then, mixed up with the scent of the little panther was that of another man. It was very different, a milder scent. Something about it seemed to stir up memories of many years past.

Now he was really confused. Why were all those man scents mixed up with that of his little offspring?

He barreled down the trail until he had passed the hollow sycamore where Anthony and Saber had sheltered, moving with renewed energy. The stronger and fresher the scent grew, the faster his feet wanted to travel.

However, he soon lost the scent of the little panther, so he turned back. He poked his head into the sycamore and found the fresh heavy scent of the kitten and that other mankind, the one that sent his memory back over the years.

The urge to hurry now intensified. He ran up the trail, taking time only occasionally to check for scent. He was well past the turnoff to the paw-paw patch before he lost the fresh scent again.

He turned sharply about, moving slower now. He checked both sides of the trail carefully until he found where the pair he was following had turned from the path.

Once again he was off. He recognized the need to move cautiously, but his feet refused to slow down.

At the paw-paw patch he found the remains of the coon carcass which Saber had feasted on. He was hungry, so he gulped down what fragments remained. Then he was back on a hot trail, one that added a new spark to his step.

At the spring, he paused for a drink. Then he started around the slope of the adjoining ridge, surprising a fox squirrel burying a nut. He could have leaped on him, but he had no time for that. The urgency to find his quarry seemed to grow with each step.

And yet, he was puzzled. Why did the scent of his little offspring and that of the other man always follow the same path? And why did the man's scent stir memories buried deep within his brain? He couldn't understand how or why, but he was trying to connect the dots.

He was nearing the crest of the ridge when he saw a coyote slinking off to his right. The scent of his little one was very hot. He had to be near. The sight of the coyote added new urgency to his mission.

He had just topped the ridge when he heard a scream. Then there was a second tiny little voice, a voice he recognized immediately. He tried frantically to double his speed.

Two great bounds landed him just behind the three coyotes advancing slowly toward the man and the kitten. They were backed up against a rock ledge, with coyotes on both sides of them. As he lunged a third time, he let out a roar that would have put a banshee to shame.

He landed on two of the coyotes, driving them to the ground, simultaneously breaking both of their backs. The third coyote that was already scrambling away as he lunged for it. He chased it a short distance, then turned back to the fray.

The two coyotes with broken backs were trying to drag themselves away with their front feet. He promptly put both of them out of their misery. The two coyotes that had been coming in on the other side of the rock had vanished like shadows when Old Crooked Toe let out his ear-splitting roar.

Now, he was confronted with the strange scene before him. Here was the little kitten he had been searching for. But with him was the owner of the other man scent. But he was a man child, a mere cub himself.

Why were they together?

Strangely, the little panther was crowding close against the leg of the child. It seemed that the man child had been trying to protect the kitten with the stick he held.

Old Crooked Toe shook his head. He turned to the nearest of the dead coyotes, picked it up by the back and shook it before throwing it into the brush. He did the same to the other coyote.

Now his attention returned once again to the man child and the kitten. Neither of them had moved. Neither of them had made a sound since they had heard his terrible roar.

The man child was still clinging to his stick. The kitten was still pressed tight against the leg of the man. Their eyes were on the old panther who had appeared so suddenly, so mysteriously.

The kitten recognized the old panther's head, but the bulk of the panther's body was much bigger than that of his mother. In his limited experience, large creatures had always presented a danger. Could he trust this creature?

Old Crooked Toe came in slowly, quietly. He touched noses with the kitten, purred softly, then backed away.

Anthony watched the actions of the big panther, mesmerized. That purr and the backing away of the old panther was a signal to the little one to go to Old Crooked Toe. Saber now moved away from Anthony slowly, taking one hesitant step, and then another. Very gently, he slid from the rock, and walked over to his father.

Anthony didn't know what to do. He stood there, not moving, not uttering a sound. The panther was big; in fact, he was enormous. And just moments before he had, almost casually, broken the backs of two coyotes in one swift motion.

Could he trust a creature like that? Maybe the two panthers would just walk away and leave him alone.

But what if they did walk away and leave him alone? After the coyote attack, he did not want to ever be alone in the wilderness again. What would he do if they did walk away and leave him?

But something was bothering the old panther. From the first time he found the odor of the man child, a thread of memory had been circling through his mind. It was faint, but it was there. A man of science might have said he was smelling the DNA of the little boy's father. Maybe so. Still, there were some dots that needed to be connected, and the old panther was trying to connect them.

Old Crooked Toe came over to the man child ever so slowly, almost cautiously. Anthony was petrified with fear; his body shivered uncontrollably, but he made no attempt to move. The panther sniffed at him and backed away. He fixed puzzled eyes on this man child he had found here, deep in the wilds of the Monongahela, a man child that had protected his little kitten.

In more than two decades of association with the humans who dwelt on the edges of the forest, Old Crooked Toe had never harmed a child. At times he had, in fact, saved them. For that matter, he had never harmed even a human adult. True, he had irritated some by feasting on their livestock, but that was a different matter entirely.

Again the old panther came over to the rock and sniffed Anthony. He then purred softly, just as he had purred to Saber, and turned away.

Anthony's body ceased to tremble when the old panther purred to him. He breathed heavily in spasms of relief.

Only now, the two panthers were walking away. What should he do? He didn't want to misread the panther's seemingly friendly purr. Then little Saber turned to look at him as if to say, "What are you waiting for? Come on."

Anthony slid from the rock and stood there, trying to decide what to do. Then, his legs made the decision for him. They started running and they didn't stop until he was close on the heels of the little panther.

CHAPTER 18

Old Crooked Toe looked back once to see that the two little ones were following him. Then he swung around a field of boulders to the other side of the ridge. He angled down the steep hill until they came out into a broad valley. It seemed to Anthony there must have been close to an acre of level land in the vale. It was an unusual sight so deep in the wilderness.

A brook babbled down its rocky bed through the valley floor, and they all paused for a drink. As Old Crooked Toe stooped to drink from the brook, Anthony noticed the old panther's left rear foot. There were two toes missing, and one of the remaining toes stuck out at an odd angle.

He had heard so much about Old Crooked Toe. Could this really be the panther that had once saved his Dad? Could this be the almost mythical creature he had day dreamed about rescuing him when he first became lost?

Those missing toes had to be the two toes that he had seen on the table beside his Dad's bed. Then there was that other toe, sticking out at a crazy angle. That toe, he had been told, was what had caused his Dad to hang the name of Old Crooked Toe on the panther.

Anthony now found himself more comfortable with this new situation he had suddenly been thrust into. In fact, he was almost jubilant. Was it real? Or, would he wake up soon and find that he was dreaming again?

Still, he felt a flicker of fear. How could this old panther get him back home? More likely, the old panther would simply lead him deeper into the depths of the Monongahela, the land that had claimed the mind and heart of Old Crooked Toe for almost three decades.

All of this would have to be solved later. Right now, with the coyote episode so fresh on his mind, Anthony had an enormous feeling of security just following along on the heels of this old panther that had so miraculously saved him and his little friend, just when all had seemed lost.

They crossed the brook and headed up out of the valley. The panther seemed to be following a straight course. He exhibited no further interest in the flush valley that Anthony felt should be excellent hunting ground.

They crossed the ridge and dropped into the next valley, then onto another ridge. Anthony and the little panther were hard pressed to keep pace with their leader, particularly up the steep slopes.

When Old Crooked Toe looked back and saw the two falling behind, he found a little wide spot on top of the ridge and paused for a brief rest. Both Anthony and Saber promptly stretched out on the leafy side of the trail.

The day was now well spent. Evening shadows were climbing onto the next ridge. The first vestige of the chill of a fall night was in the air.

Anthony wondered just how far into the night they would travel. The way his legs were aching, he hoped not long. But he was determined to keep up, regardless of how far they went before they found shelter for the night.

After their brief rest, they swung around the next ridge. For the first time, Old Crooked Toe seemed to be departing from his straight course. As they came around the side of the next ridge, Anthony saw a series of broken cliffs.

The old panther now became more cautious. Twice, he paused, scanning the slope before them.

Anthony suspected that they were approaching one of the old panther's secret hideouts. He had once done a school paper based on one of the stories his Dad had relayed to him about visiting one of the old panther's secret retreats.

They approached the largest of the cliff formations. As they got closer, Anthony could make out a cavity beneath the rock.

When Old Crooked Toe poked his head into the cavity, loud screeches erupted from within the cavern. Then Anthony saw two wildcats leap out into the open.

Old Crooked Toe lunged at the cats. Being smaller and quicker, they leaped nimbly away, turning to spar with their antagonist. They would not give up their shelter peaceably.

It was a game many of the wildcat tribe had played with Old Crooked Toe over the years. But when the old panther lunged out again and one of his great forepaws landed close to one of the wildcats, they decided that retreat was the better choice. They slunk off around the hill, grumbling to themselves.

Old Crooked Toe promptly checked out the cavity, then brought his two wards inside.

Anthony was glad for a chance to lay down and rest. Little Saber also seemed glad for a break. He lost no time in finding a nest in the leaves, and was soon fast asleep.

Anthony had no way of knowing how long the little panther had been alone in the wilderness. But with their-new found security, little Saber would rest more peaceably tonight than he had for possibly many nights.

Anthony had, at times during his sojourn in the wilderness, felt some satisfaction in being able to survive in the wilds of the Monongahela. But all such feelings had vanished when he faced the pack of coyotes with only a walking stick to protect his little companion.

The new security that Anthony felt had not come just from the fact that the panther had saved him and the kitten. It had been galvanized by the knowledge that the panther was truly Old Crooked Toe himself. He was the real thing. He was the panther who had become a legend while he was still young. And Anthony was convinced that he was still the stuff of legend, after seeing him dispense with a pack of five coyotes in the blink of an eye.

When Anthony had rested some, he realized that he was hungry. He had eaten some of his paw-paws before the coyotes came along, but he still had two in the plastic bag under his shirt. He decided to eat one of the fruits and save one for breakfast.

Little Saber had stuffed himself on the coon carcass earlier that morning, so he would be fine for the night. Of the three, only Old Crooked Toe was really hurting for nourishment. In his haste to find his offspring he had neglected searching for food. He had, on more than one occasion let an easy kill get away from him.

For the first time since he had become lost, Anthony was relaxed. He enjoyed hearing the night come in. They were still in the tall timber where the land had not been cut over. There was a host of wood thrushes, and they set the forest to ringing. Then, their raucous calling ended, followed by that sacred time known as the twilight hour.

Anthony fell asleep listening to the rasping of the katydids. If there were any frightening sounds during the night, they did not disturb his rest.

CHAPTER 19

Anthony did not awaken until the sun was already peeping over the mountains to the east. Sometime during the night both Anthony and Saber had moved over against the old panther's back for warmth. Old Crooked Toe did not move until he felt it was time for the three of them to get on the trail.

Saber and Anthony were rested and ready to go when their leader came out of the shelter and purred softly. They set off, the pair eagerly following close on the old panther's heels. Saber, as usual, was constantly on the lookout for something to nibble on, searching for an insect that failed to scramble away hastily enough.

Old Crooked Toe now retraced his steps of last evening until he was back on course. They went straight down the steep incline until they were in a draw, where they found a bubbly little spring. They all paused for a drink.

Anthony dug his lone paw-paw from the plastic bag in his shirt. During the night the fruit had gotten smashed. When he tried to get it out of the bag he dropped it in the dirt, so there was no breakfast for him. Saber found a frog in the branch, which he promptly gulped down. Then they were on the go again, to wherever it was that Old Crooked Toe was taking them.

When they climbed the next ridge they came to a mountain range that ran north and south. The old panther came onto a wide bench that ran along the side of the incline. This proved a break from climbing up and down the steep hills for the two little ones.

It was well past noon before the old panther slowed his pace. Anthony noticed that Old Crooked Toe kept looking down the ridge. Curiosity got the better of Anthony, so he darted over where he could see down below. What he saw was a wide valley, with many open spaces. He thought he could see a couple deer in the open spaces. He ran to catch up with the two panthers.

Shortly, Old Crooked Toe paused. The two little ones sank down to rest. They were both tired and hungry. Anthony was famished. He had eaten only one piece of fruit last night and none today. And the pace the big cat had set for them had begun to tell on both Anthony and Saber.

The old panther walked over to the brink of the bench and studied the situation down below. Then he cruised out ahead for about a hundred yards. There he found what he was looking for.

He turned and purred. It was a different sound from his previous utterances earlier in the morning. Saber climbed off the trail and hid behind some bushes, flattening down in the leafy cover.

Anthony interpreted this purr as an order to hide and stay put. He, too hid behind the same bushes with the little panther.

In a flash Old Crooked Toe was gone. A flicker of fear passed over Anthony.

What if the coyotes came again? Or maybe that pair of wildcats? He could only hope that Old Crooked Toe would be close enough to come to their rescue if they needed him.

Tired, hungry and weary, the two little ones soaked up the warm sun that bathed the mountain about them. Soon they were both fast asleep. They did not realize that it was more than two hours before Old Crooked Toe emerged over the rim of the bench.

The old panther had taken time to stuff himself on his kill before he came back. Now he carried a full quarter of venison, skinned and ready for his two wards. He found a clean place in the leaves and laid the meat down. Then he found a place to rest, licking the drippings from his front feet and legs.

Saber lost no time in sailing into the fresh meat. Anthony watched Saber spitting and growling as he tore off bits of meat and gulped them down half chewed.

Anthony was hungry. In fact he was famished. He dug in his hip pocket and came out with an acorn. He took out his knife and opened the nut, then nibbled a bit. It was more bitter than he had remembered. He threw it down.

From now on, all they would have to eat would likely be panther food. Could he eat it? There were no more paw-paws. There would be no more wild plumbs. There would be no more apples. He would have one choice --panther food, or go hungry.

He wanted to get home again. He wanted to survive. And to do so he had to keep up his strength. So what other choice was there? He knew none.

He opened his knife again and moved over to the venison. He lifted a piece of red meat and cut it off with his knife. He looked at it only briefly then stuck it in his mouth. It was still warm. It was sweet.

With Saber chewing on one end of the quarter and Anthony working on the other, the two little ones ate until they were both sated. Soon it was time to sleep again. Anthony wiped his knife and fingers on his pants leg.

What a story he would have to tell his friends -- that is, if he ever got home.

Old Crooked Toe rose up and carried the remains of the venison over the edge of the bench, burying it in the leaves. Purring to his charges, he set off around the next bend. They had travelled less than a hundred yards when the old panther turned from the level ground and set off up the side of a steep draw.

They were soon within sight of a sheer rock wall. It was close to twenty feet high and its base was shrouded in a dense thicket of brush.

Old Crooked Toe led his charges behind the thicket. Suddenly, they emerged beneath a great overhang of lichen covered sandstone cliffs. At the far end of the overhang the waters of a spring ran hardly a dozen feet until they dropped off into a rock-filled trench into the valley far below.

They drank their fill. Anthony looked over the trench to see where the spring water went. He watched the clear mountain water tumble down the trench to the valley. Anthony hoped they were dropping down out of the mountains, maybe even toward Cave Creek Valley. It was a long way down to the bottom of the ravine. There, the little tumbling branch joined a much larger stream

No, he thought, they were still well up in the highlands. It was something he would have fitful dreams about before the night was over.

With the three of them comfortably full, and weary from so much travel, they didn't wait for the night to come in. They each selected a spot, curled up and went to sleep beneath the great rock overhang. Later in the night, when the wildcats screamed and the coyotes yapped, nobody heard them.

CHAPTER 20

Old Crooked Toe was the first to stir the following morning. He stretched and yawned, letting out a healthy yowl. The two little ones followed him up soon after. The sun had not yet peeped over the mountains. Everyone sipped a bit of water. They were ready for whatever this new day would bring.

Anthony had kept count of his days in the wilderness. He was now on day seven. He wondered what was going on back in Cave Creek Valley. Certainly his parents had been looking for him. But they had not found him.

It had been a long time since he had seen or heard the helicopter. Apparently, the searchers had given up using it, or they were looking in entirely the wrong area. Certainly they hadn't given up the search completely, had they?

As for himself, he was still lost. And right now, for all he knew , the three of them could well be heading deeper into the heart of that great forest.

Old Crooked Toe still seemed to be on a mission. He wound his way back around the hillside to the bench they had followed yesterday. He turned to his right and headed out the bench.

They had travelled only a short distance until the bench swung around, ending in a deep draw. Crossing the draw was a well packed game trail. Old

Crooked Toe began a gentle descent into the draw.

Anthony watched the old panther closely. Maybe, just maybe they were coming down out of the high country, but he didn't want to get his hopes up.

For the past six days, every hope Anthony had harbored was dashed before the day was over. He didn't need another such day. Now, as they dropped down into the draw, he found himself hoping again.

When they came to a broad valley and turned right, Old Crooked Toe was, according to the sun, on that same course he had followed for the past two days. He certainly knew where he was going, even if Anthony didn't.

Anthony was surprised that he was not hungry. Maybe he was learning why the old panther, and his kind, could go without food for some days after they gorged themselves. Maybe cooking that sweet red meat took away some of its staying power. What a tale he would tell if he ever got home. When that day came, he would lay it on heavy. Not by stretching the truth; he wouldn't need to. Something like this didn't happen every day back home.

Everything was going well, until they rounded a bend in the trail and ran smack into a black bear. He wasn't one of those giant black brutes, but he was a fair sized young rascal with a mean disposition, a cocky creature who was feeling his oats.

Old Crooked Toe paid no attention to the bear. He simply plodded along as though the rascal was not there. Then the bear reared up and threatened the old panther with one of his heavy forearms.

Old Crooked Toe feinted. He got the bear to strike and miss. He then darted in and struck the bear a heavy blow with his right forepaw. He caught the black rascal just back of the ear and sent him rolling.

The bear came back, now charging on all four feet. Again Old Crooked Toe leaped aside, then attacked, sending the rascal rolling for a second time.

Now fully infuriated, the bear charged a third time. Perhaps he had never encountered a panther before. If so, today he was to learn a hard lesson. For this time, Old Crooked Toe leaped onto his back and sank his teeth deep into the bear's neck.

The bear let out a squall, shook himself free and loped on down the trail to wherever he was going in the first place.

Anthony was amazed at the old panther. He showed no emotion, no apparent anger. He simply turned back to the trail and moved along as though nothing exciting had happened.

After this last encounter, Anthony was beginning to see that he had been wise to avoid those hard packed game trails. He couldn't wait to tell his friends about that bear fight. Maybe he wouldn't exaggerate, but then he certainly wouldn't play it down. In fact, it would make a very good subject for another school paper.

Along about mid-morning Old Crooked Toe paused to let the little ones rest. Saber stretched out on the trail and was soon fast asleep. Anthony just flopped down and continued to dwell on where they were and where they were going. After that last descent he had gotten his hopes up, maybe only a little bit. But it was encouraging.

When Old Crooked Toe got to his feet and started out again, he increased his pace to the point that Anthony and Saber had trouble keeping up. But keep up they did. Neither of them wanted to be very far from that big panther. He was their only security in this wild land. They would keep up somehow, regardless of how fast he went.

After his encounter with the coyotes yesterday, and now the fight with the bear, Anthony didn't want to ever be left alone in the wilderness again. Any thoughts that he could make it on his own had vanished from his mind.

In the afternoon the old panther selected a rocky little trail that wound around a set of small ridges. Soon, Anthony saw a clump of bushes with yellow fruit hanging on them.

Sure enough, here was a tree full of paw paws, hanging right over the trail. Fully ripe mountain bananas!

Even if Anthony was going to eat panther food from now on, he still wanted a few of those yellow fruits.

He climbed onto a rock on the side of the trail, but he was unable to reach any of the paw-paws. He reached up,grabbing a limb that held some of those bright golden gems, but when he tried to pull it down, the limb broke.

Anthony and the paw paw limb went spiraling down the steep bank. He landed on his left leg about ten feet down the incline in a pile of boulders. His first knowledge that he might be seriously hurt was a sharp pain in his left leg, just above the ankle.

When Anthony tried to get up he discovered that he had broken his left leg. The pain was severe, and it was a moment before he realized that the panthers were moving rapidly away down the trail, and he was being left behind.

"Help," Anthony yelled.

When Old Crooked Toe heard the cry, he looked back. The man child was not following him. This was the same man child who had stood there on the rock with his walking stick in hand, ready to defend Old Crooked Toe's offspring. He could not leave him behind.

He turned back up the trail at once, and found Anthony at the foot of the steep, rocky bank. He searched for a place where he could get down through the rocks to the boy. When he finally worked his way down to Anthony, he appeared at a loss as to what to do next.

He paced up and down beside the boy, purring to him. But that brought no movement from Anthony.

The old panther tried to lift Anthony by his shirt collar, but when that ripped he let go and backed away.

Old Crooked Toe stood beside Anthony for close to a minute, trying to decide what to do. Then he lay down beside him with his back against the the man child.

Anthony realized that the panther was trying to get him on his back. So he hastily removed his belt from his pants and buckled it around the neck of Old

Crooked Toe. He then threw his right leg over the animal's back and gripped the belt with both hands.

When the panther stood up, Anthony found himself on the back of his rescuer. It wasn't the most comfortable position he had ever been in, but he was off the ground. And he now knew that the panther would not go off and leave him alone with a broken leg.

As Old Crooked Toe clawed his way back up the steep incline, Anthony found himself clinging to the belt around the old panther's neck as he climbed almost straight up. Finally, the panther was safely back on the trail with his heavy load.

They started down the trail once more. The old panther's pace was slowed by his heavy load, so much so that Saber found it easy to keep up.

Anthony looked back up the trail as they moved away. He could still see those ripe yellow fruits. What had he done to himself? He had not gotten even one paw paw. To make matters worse, he had lost his walking stick.

How would he ever get home with a broken leg? And how would he survive here in the wilderness trying to get around on one leg? The panther could not carry him all the time. He had to hunt and he couldn't do that with Anthony on his back. What if he encountered another bear on the trail? What would happen to him if another fight ensued?

These were just a few of the questions running through Anthony's mind as they moved along the trail. The old panther, plodding along with his heavy load, was still on the same course that he had kept for the last two days. Twice, during the afternoon, he paused, bellying down to rest for a few minutes. Then he was back on the trail.

Anthony found that when he let his left leg down and pulled it forward so the lower leg was straight down, the pain was not as severe. Yet it still hurt. If he was back home, right now he would be taking pain pills.

Evening shadows began to climb up the hills, and still Old Crooked Toe walked wearily on. Soon, he paused and bellied down to rest. While he rested, night shadows came swiftly down the steep slopes about them, and they were immediately enveloped in night.

When would they stop, Anthony wondered. Where would they spend the night? How would he manage with the broken leg?

He was weary. He was desperately tired. How would he ever get a drink of water? And he still hadn't get any of those golden yellow paw-paws.

PART IV
CHAPTER 21

Back in Cave Creek Valley, the past week had been a nightmare for the Reeves family. It all started on the night of the great community gathering, when Anthony did not return home after the festivities. Ken and Katie thought that he was off somewhere with his friends. After all, he had a new camera to show off. He was probably taking lots of pictures. There seemed to be little reason for concern, until darkness came.

Then it was past dinner time, but Anthony wasn't there. Katie called all of his friends that she could think of. They all told the same story. No one had seen him since the hike earlier in the day. Pam Lee remembered seeing Anthony wander away from the group as he tried to get some bird pictures. But she did not remember seeing him rejoin the walk.

Katie was frantic. Kennie tried to calm her. Their son would be wandering in any minute now. But he didn't wander in. Neither did Katie calm down.

With his own fear growing, Kennie tried to maintain his composure, and at the same time, allay Katie's fears.

At last, the facts outweighed hope. Anthony was not to be found anywhere in Cave Creek Valley. Anthony was lost.

Kennie went to work on the phone. He called his friends to set up search parties. He needed the help of some of the older residents who knew something about the lay of the land in those vast reaches of the Monongahela Forest.

First he called Cory Long, who said that, of course, he would come. Yes, he would have no trouble finding two more to make up his search party. Then Kennie called Elliot Conner, who said he would assemble and lead another search party. Those two groups, with Kennie and two more people to make up his team, would comprise the three search teams.

They all agreed to meet in one hour at Old Skid Road. Both Kennie and Katie wanted the search to start as soon as possible. And Katie let it be known, in no uncertain terms, that she would go with Kennie.

"You should stay here by the phone," Kennie insisted. "Suppose someone should call with a message concerning Anthony. One of us should be here to take that call."

That worked, and Katie agreed to stay home. So the search was set to begin.

"There is something else you can do that might help," Kennie told Katie. "If you would call the National Guard, they might send a helicopter to help with the search."

The three teams met at the foot of the mountain as planned. Soon all nine were climbing up Old Skid Road to the top of the mountain.

If Anthony was anywhere on Sugar Maple Mountain, he would know his way home. So they moved on down to the little brook that separated Sugar

Maple Mountain from the Monongahela Forest.

Here they laid their plans for the search. First off, and very importantly, they would stay in touch by calls. Kennie let it be known that he did not want any more lost persons to deal with.

"One is quite enough to deal with at a time," he said.

Kennie had brought his father's old cow horn call. He spaced the searchers and gave the order to move out.

They searched the area north of the main game trail that led deep into the forest. They started by lining up along the little brook that formed the line between the forest and Sugar Maple Mountain.

Kennie left one man about one hundred feet from the game trail, then he led the rest of the group up the brook, dropping off a man about every one hundred feet until they were all spread out.

Next, he sounded the horn, and everyone started moving away from the brook. They stayed in touch by each frequently calling Anthony's name. In this manner, they covered a wide swath.

The going was slower than they had hoped. Those in the upper end of the search group had much climbing to do.

It was well past midnight when they had gone well beyond the point where Anthony could possibly have travelled before night caught him. Kennie sounded the horn for everyone to halt in place.

Now Kennie gathered his men as he returned to the main game trail. Here again it took more time than expected. The going at night was more difficult than it would have been in daylight.

"Now, we will use the same plan to search the other side of the game trail as we go back." Kennie said.

They would never know that one of them had already passed within fifty yards of the little boy who was so tired and sleeping so soundly that he did not hear his name called.

They reached the back side of Sugar Maple Mountain well before the break of day. Tired and deeply disappointed, they decided to go home, get something to eat and rest until noon. Then they would reassemble at Old Skid Road.

But there was a problem. Cory Long had to go to work, as would one other member of his team. They could help during the night, but would not be able to help search during the day. The total search team was reduced to seven.

What no one could understand was how Anthony could have, in such a short time, gone beyond the vast area they had searched. And, of course, he had not.

Katie had called some friends over to help her pass the hours away. They had been long hours. The first frantic night of coping with a lost child was over.

Katie was devastated, yet she managed to fix up something for Kennie to eat. After eating, Kennie tried to settle down, and get some much needed rest before the next search.

The two of them talked for almost an hour before Kennie dozed off. Katie told Kennie that she had called the Commander at the National Guard. He had not only agreed to send a helicopter, but he had made a special trip to Cave Creek Valley to get oriented with the area, and determine where to search.

The Commander reported later that day, while Kennie slept, that the first search had found nothing, but he would send the aircraft out the following day to search a wider area.

Katie was unable to sleep. She got up from bed and tried to busy herself. Her friends had gone home at the break of day, so Katie called them to report the dismal results of the first day of search.

CHAPTER 22

The next morning, Katie woke Kennie. She had fixed a couple sandwiches and a bottle of water for his back pack. Then they had a brief prayer session.

The helicopter came back and did a wider, more extensive search. But of course, this time he was searching well beyond the limits of Anthony's travels.

Kennie's search efforts were likewise fruitless. By the third day, Katie was unable to eat or to sleep, and she became violently ill. The Reverend Jacob Chambers, who pastored the local church, had come twice to pray with Katie and try to comfort her. Twice Kennie had to give up the search to take her to the clinic.

The number of searchers continued to decrease. Even though an occasional new volunteer joined them, the extent of searches was reduced.

When a week had passed with no search results, Reverend Chambers called for a community prayer session.

Word was passed that at the ringing of the church bell, the faithful were to gather in the church. At two o'clock on the seventh day, the church bell rang loud and clear. Within half an hour the church was filled with residents of the valley. Some came simply because they were members of the congregation, others because of sympathy for the grieving Reeves family.

Reverend Chambers, spoke briefly about the reason the gathering, then offered up a prayer. His prayer was followed by brief prayers from two of the church Elders.

Someone in the crowd shouted, "Where is Agnes Long?"

Someone else took up the call, followed by other voices.

Kennie and Katie were standing off to one side of the crowd. Katie looked up at Kennie.

"Where have we been?" she asked.

"I've been out in the woods when I haven't been trying to comfort you," Kennie said.

"That's not what I mean," Katie said. "Why haven't we gone to Agnes and have her pray for us?"

"Now I see what you mean," Kennie said. "I have been so busy and so worried I haven't been able to think straight."

Cory and Agnes were standing over on the other side of the crowd. Agnes, still having trouble getting around after her wreck, was supported by Cory.

Reverend Chambers waved Cory and Agnes to come forward. They immediately started toward the pulpit.

"Kennie," Katie said. "Help Cory get Agnes up the steps to the pulpit."

Kennie and Katie both hurried to help Cory.

When Agnes was stable, they backed away.

Agnes turned her face up to the Heavens that seemed to hover so close above the gathering. She lifted her right hand up over her head and prayed: "Our Father which art in Heaven, hallowed be Thy name. Thy Kingdom come, Thy will be done on Earth as it is in Heaven.

"We come to You humbly, God, admitting our unworthiness and asking Your mercy once again.

"Please God, bring our little lost boy home safe.

"We ask this in the name of Your Son, our loving Savior, Jesus Christ. And may the Glory, Majesty and Honor be unto You now and forever. Amen."

Kennie and Cory helped Agnes down the steps, and Katie joined them for a brief visit. While they talked, other friends came by to give their best wishes, to assure them that all would be well, and to tell them that their boy would soon be home.

When Kennie got Katie home, he was aware that she was terribly stressed. What she had expected from the prayer session, he was not sure. Maybe she expected some immediate results, which had not happened.

Kennie, masking his own concerns, and at the same time wanting to console Katie, felt lost for words of comfort.

"We'll just have to give the prayer session time to work," he insisted. "We'll just have faith. That is the key -- Faith."

"Time," Katie said. "A week of fruitless search and we want more time. We might just as well face facts, Kennie. Our boy is no longer out there. Something terribly bad has happened to him. If he was still out there, someone would have found him by now."

"What you say makes sense," Kenny replied. "But we must not forget that the Monongahela covers an enormous area. As for me, I am about ready to call off all of the search missions, and give God time to answer that prayer that Agnes made."

"That old panther which we let out of the trap a long time ago has probably found our boy and eaten him," Katie said.

"Don't be so gruesome," Kennie replied. "Get such thoughts out of your mind."

"Out of my mind?" Katie said. "When our boy has been out there in the wilderness for a full week and no one has seen him, or even found a sign to indicate that he is alive? And a helicopter has spent two days searching without a sign of him? How do I keep from thinking the worst?"

After some further discussion, Kennie suggested that he would do his chores. Then they could talk some more while they prepared dinner. So he took his milk pail and headed for the barn.

When he returned, Kennie found Katie still sitting where she was when they had returned from the prayer session. She had a towel over her face and was sobbing softly.

Kennie took some left-overs from the refrigerator, warmed them and opened a can of vegetable soup. He asked Katie to join him at the table.

"I'm not hungry," Katie replied. "I don't feel like eating."

Kennie ate a few bites, but he had no appetite either. Then he called Cory Long.

"I'm sorry to bother you at this late hour," Kennie said. "But would you and Agnes mind coming over and helping me try to calm Katie? This has been a terribly stressful week for her and I need your help."

"We'll be right over," Cory replied.

Kennie hung up the phone. "I'll leave the food on the table in case you may want something later," he said.

"Not tonight," came the reply. "No food tonight. When I can get myself together I think I will go to bed."

Kennie cleared the table as he anxiously awaited the coming of Agnes Long. There was something about her great Faith that made Agnes' presence soothing, even when she was not talking. And Kennie needed her presence now.

CHAPTER 23

When the bell rang, Kennie rushed to the door. After greeting Agnes and Cory, Kennie stood back while Agnes walked over to Katie.

"Where's my friend?" Agnes said. "My dear friend who should be anxiously awaiting the return of her lost son?"

Katie dropped the towel from her face. Her cheeks were flushed and tear-stained. She tried to smile, but that failed.

"After the good prayer session we had," Agnes said. "I expected to find you in great spirits."

"Great spirits, when my son has been lost in the wilderness for a full week?" Katie replied. "And now he is spending another night alone out there in the cold and dark. Alone with all of those wild, dangerous animals.

"I told Kennie that I expect that old panther has already found him and ate him. And if he has, it is my fault. It was me who struck the gun up and saved that panther's life when Kennie was about to kill him. I wish now I had let him die."

"Had you planned to do that?" Agnes asked.

"No," Katie said. "Not at all,".

"You did it on an impulse. God led you to do it," Agnes said. "When I saw the gun on top of the trap that day I asked God to not let Kennie kill the old panther. He answered that prayer by using you.

"We all belong to God, everybody, every animal, everything. St. John tells us that. 'All things were made by God,' and 'Without Him was not anything made that was made.' We are God's to use as He needs us. You were led to do what you did. Someday, you will understand why. And when you do, you will be glad that you did. There were lots of people who wanted Old Crooked Toe killed before he saved my children from that pack of wild dogs. If they had succeeded, where would my children be now? Just think about it. Arick would not be in college. He would be filling a grave on the knoll in behind the church. And Faith would not be a junior in High School. She would be in another grave beside Arick."

"But Anthony, if he is still alive, is now spending another night alone out there in the wilderness," Katie said. "He has to be hungry. And he has to be cold. And he most certainly has to be frightened. I would be, if I was out there alone in the night, without food, without company, without shelter."

"You have good reason to be stressed," Agnes said. "But adversity is an essential part of life. It brings us back to God when we have unconsciously drifted away. It brings families together, cities together, even entire nations together.

"Adversity alerts us once again to our need for God's help, God's Love and God's guidance. And there is where faith comes in. We must not let adversity shake our faith.

"Now," Agnes continued. "I want you to repeat after me -- God will take care of my son."

"God will take care of my son," Katie said.

"That was terrible," Agnes said. "You just said words. There was no meaning, no feeling in them. I want you to stand up and say that again, loud and clear. Loud enough that it will ring in the ears of Kennie and Cory out in the kitchen, and I want you to believe what you are saying."

"GOD WILL TAKE CARE OF MY SON!" Katie shouted.

"That was better," Agnes said. "Now I want you to repeat after me, again loud and clear -- God will bring my son home."

"You're treating me like a child," Katie said.

"Not at all," Agnes replied. "I want you to think like an adult who has faith in God and faith in prayer."

"GOD WILL BRING MY SON HOME!" Katie shouted.

As Katie finished, there came a faint cry, "Help!"

No one knew where it came from. It was followed by a scream so loud that it almost seemed to be in the room with them. The windows rattled and the door shook. Kennie and Cory, who were seated at the Kitchen table, jumped to their feet.

Kennie raced to the door, threw it open and switched on the light. For a moment he stood, transfixed. Then, with his gaze still held by what he saw, he waved his hand behind him and shouted, " Katie! Katie, come quick!"

Katie, supported by Agnes' arm around her shoulders, came running. There, trying to sit up on the back of Old Crooked Toe, after a long and hazardous ride, she saw her little lost boy. A panther cub stood at Old Crooked Toe's side.

Everybody eased slowly out onto the porch, trying not to spook the old panther. No one spoke.

"I need help," Anthony called. "I have a broken leg."

Kennie eased down the steps. He walked slowly over to Old Crooked Toe and lifted Anthony from his back. He carried the lost boy over to the porch and handed him up to Cory.

Kennie wanted desperately to thank his old friend. But how did you thank a panther?

"Katie," he called. " Katie, bring that fresh roast from the fridge."

Katie, who was hovering over her son on the couch, called to Cory.

"I'm busy with my son, Cory," she said. "Would you please take Kennie the roast he wants? It's in the meat drawer in the fridge."

Then she turned back to Anthony.

"What did you say, baby?" she asked her son.

"Mommy," Anthony said. "You remember that story you told me about how you saved the life of the old panther? Well, just you wait until I tell you what he did for me and my friend Saber!"

When Cory brought the roast, Kennie took it and turned. But the old panther was not there. Neither was the little panther. The light illuminated the yard but no panther was visible anywhere.

Old Crooked Toe had completed his mission. He had finally connected the dots and knew where the little lost boy belonged. Having delivered him, he and his little offspring were already racing back through the night to that fabulous land of their birth.

Although Old Crooked Toe would probably never return to Cave Creek Valley again, the spirit of the old panther was destined to live forever in the deep dark aisles of the mythical, magical Monongahela.

www.ingramcontent.com/pod-product-compliance
Lightning Source LLC
Chambersburg PA
CBHW071308130626
46556CB00004B/1523